WLE Short Stories 5

Sinister and Supernatural Stories

Chosen by Richard Adams

Ward Lock Educational

ISBN 0 7062 3668 8   hardback
      0 7062 3667 x   paperback

First published 1978
Reprinted 1980

Set in 12 on 13 point Bembo
by Computacomp (UK) Limited
and printed by Biddles Ltd, Guildford, Surrey
for Ward Lock Educational
116 Baker Street, London W1M 2BB
A member of the Pentos Group
Made in Great Britain

Contents

This collection
– and especially *Poor Ash* – is for
TIM PEARCE

Acknowledgments

The editor and publishers would like to thank the following for their permission to reproduce copyright material: George Mackay Brown for 'Brig-o-Dread'; 'Thus I refute Beelzy' by John Collier, reprinted by permission of A. D. Peters and Company; Roald Dahl for 'Royal Jelly' from *Kiss Kiss* © 1959 by Roald Dahl, published by Michael Joseph and Penguin Books; Daphne du Maurier for 'The Birds' from *The Apple Tree* published by Gollancz; Pamela Hansford-Johnson and Curtis Brown for 'The Empty Schoolroom' from *That Uncertain Feeling* published by New English Library.

Every effort has been made to trace owners of copyright material, but in some cases this has not proved possible. The publishers would be glad to hear from any further copyright owners of material reproduced in *WLE Short Stories 5: Sinister and Supernatural Stories*.

Introduction

The world of the supernatural is a wide world. It presents its full front to a horror-hungry public by way of the crowded shelves of bookshops, newsagents and supermarkets, of the cinema and of the 'late-night-movie' slot on television. It ranges from Count Dracula's Transylvania – with its gothic castles, its dungeon-laboratories, its mist-mantled graveyards – to realms beyond space and time, where the unsuspecting traveller will find himself, as like as not, confronted with mind-projections, haunted orbiters and galactic monsters.

Somewhere about half-way between these extremes lies a sizeable tract of supernatural fiction that, brushing aside clichés of the ancient crypt and abandoned satellite order, takes as its starting point the everyday world of everyday people. Far from being the disadvantage it might at first seem, such familiarity of setting is often the very key to success of this particular brand of 'chiller', centring as it does on the infinite capacity for fear and fantasy that exists in the human imagination and in the world which surrounds and stimulates it. It is from this broad area that the majority of the stories in the present collection derives. Two of them, for example, are set against innocent school backgrounds; two snuggle comfortably in the bosoms of unexceptional suburban families; two focus on landscapes most readily associated with sunny carefree holidays, while the remaining one concerns an unpretentious English country house on a spectacularly serene summer's evening.

The acute sense of unease, of foreboding, finally of blank terror in these stories and the impact of the situations and events they describe depend utterly on their ability to make us believe that they just *could*, just *might* happen to us. The thrill, the nervous shudder which they produce in the reader fascinate as well as trouble him because they spring from totally unexpected origins – from a flock of birds, for instance, from a small baby, from the very bricks and mortar of a house – and because they are played upon and developed by the art of a calculating storyteller. They are born of a combination of the simple and the sinister in the minds of their writers.

Though its effect is perhaps ultimately more sensational than those of other stories in the book, *Poor Ash* may serve to illustrate what I mean. It is based on my experiences while staying, as a thirteen-year-old boy, in the house of some relatives in a small village in the south of England. I remember being unable to sleep, not because of the sultriness of the summer's night, I think, so much as because something unidentifiable about my bedroom was worrying me. The same night, the family dog – an elderly, portly animal who had never performed an insane act in his life – tried to jump through a closed window downstairs. I do not know whether my sleeplessness was in any way related to this incident, but together they made sufficient impression on me to set me writing, many years later, in *Poor Ash*, about a house with a life of its own – and not only a life, but a mind and an appetite. The ideas developed quickly and with disturbing logic – rather, I imagine, as did Daphne du Maurier's in the writing of her now famous imaginative account of the day that the birds started to make war on the human race, or Roald Dahl's in the creation of his brilliantly amusing but uncomfortable theory as to what might happen if you were to raise a baby on a diet of royal jelly. These two tales are undoubtedly the cornerstones of what I hope, despite its lack of blatant sensationalism, will prove to be for its readers a suitably disconcerting collection.

The Birds

Daphne du Maurier

On December the third the wind changed overnight and it was winter. Until then the autumn had been mellow, soft. The leaves had lingered on the trees, golden red, and the hedgerows were still green. The earth was rich where the plough had turned it.

Nat Hocken, because of a war-time disability, had a pension and did not work full-time at the farm. He worked three days a week, and they gave him the lighter jobs: hedging, thatching, repairs to the farm buildings.

Although he was married, with children, his was a solitary disposition; he liked best to work alone. It pleased him when he was given a bank to build up, or a gate to mend at the far end of the peninsula, where the sea surrounded the farm land on either side. Then, at midday, he would pause and eat the pasty that his wife had baked for him, and sitting on the cliff's edge would watch the birds. Autumn was best for this, better than spring. In spring the birds flew inland, purposeful, intent; they knew where they were bound, the rhythm and ritual of their life brooked no delay. In autumn those that had not migrated overseas but remained to pass the winter were caught up in the same driving urge, but because migration was denied them followed a pattern of their own. Great flocks of them came to the peninsula, restless, uneasy, spending themselves in motion; now wheeling, circling in the sky, now settling to feed on the rich new-turned soil, but even when they fed it was as though they did so without hunger, without desire. Restlessness drove them to the skies again.

Black and white, jackdaw and gull, mingled in strange

partnership, seeking some sort of liberation, never satisfied, never still. Flocks of starlings, rustling like silk, flew to fresh pasture, driven by the same necessity of movement, and the smaller birds, the finches and the larks, scattered from tree to hedge as if compelled.

Nat watched them, and he watched the sea-birds too. Down in the bay they waited for the tide. They had more patience. Oyster-catchers, redshank, sanderling, and curlew watched by the water's edge; as the slow sea sucked at the shore and then withdrew, leaving the strip of seaweed bare and the shingle churned, the sea-birds raced and ran upon the beaches. Then that same impulse to flight seized upon them too. Crying, whistling, calling, they skimmed the placid sea and left the shore. Make haste, make speed, hurry and begone; yet where, and to what purpose? The restless urge of autumn, unsatisfying, sad, had put a spell upon them and they must flock, and wheel, and cry; they must spill themselves of motion before winter came.

Perhaps, thought Nat, munching his pasty by the cliff's edge, a message comes to the birds in autumn, like a warning. Winter is coming. Many of them perish. And like people who, apprehensive of death before their time, drive themselves to work or folly, the birds do likewise.

The birds had been more restless than ever this fall of the year, the agitation more marked because the days were still. As the tractor traced its path up and down the western hills, the figure of the farmer silhouetted on the driving-seat, the whole machine and the man upon it would be lost momentarily in the great cloud of wheeling, crying birds. There were many more than usual, Nat was sure of this. Always, in autumn, they followed the plough, but not in great flocks like these, nor with such clamour.

Nat remarked upon it, when hedging was finished for the day. 'Yes,' said the farmer, 'there are more birds about than usual; I've noticed it too. And daring, some of them, taking no notice of the tractor. One or two gulls came so close to my head this afternoon I thought they'd knock my cap off! As it was, I could scarcely see what I was doing, when they were overhead and I had the sun in my eyes. I have a notion the weather will change. It will be a hard winter. That's why the birds are restless.'

Nat, tramping home across the fields and down the lane to his cottage, saw the birds still flocking over the western hills, in the last glow of the sun. No wind, and the grey sea calm and full. Campion in bloom yet in the hedges, and the air mild. The farmer was right, though, and it was that night the weather turned. Nat's bedroom faced east. He woke just after two and heard the wind in the chimney. Not the storm and bluster of a sou'westerly gale, bringing the rain, but east wind, cold and dry. It sounded hollow in the chimney, and a loose slate rattled on the roof. Nat listened, and he could hear the sea roaring in the bay. Even the air in the small bedroom had turned chill: a draught came under the skirting of the door, blowing upon the bed. Nat drew the blanket round him, leant closer to the back of his sleeping wife, and stayed wakeful, watchful, aware of misgiving without cause.

Then he heard the tapping on the window. There was no creeper on the cottage walls to break loose and scratch upon the pane. He listened, and the tapping continued until, irritated by the sound, Nat got out of bed and went to the window. He opened it, and as he did so something brushed his hand, jabbing at his knuckles, grazing the skin. The he saw the flutter of the wings and it was gone, over the roof, behind the cottage.

It was a bird, what kind of bird he could not tell. The wind must have driven it to shelter on the sill.

He shut the window and went back to bed, but feeling his knuckles wet put his mouth to the scratch. The bird had drawn blood. Frightened, he supposed, and bewildered, the bird, seeking shelter, had stabbed at him in the darkness. Once more he settled himself to sleep.

Presently the tapping came again, this time more forceful, more insistent, and now his wife woke at the sound, and turning in the bed said to him, 'See to the window, Nat, it's rattling.'

'I've already seen to it,' he told her, 'there's some bird there, trying to get in. Can't you hear the wind? It's blowing from the east, driving the birds to shelter.'

'Send them away,' she said, 'I can't sleep with that noise.'

He went to the window for the second time, and now when he opened it there was not one bird upon the sill but half a dozen; they flew straight into his face, attacking him.

He shouted, striking out at them with his arms, scattering them; like the first one, they flew over the roof and disappeared. Quickly he let the window fall and latched it.

'Did you hear that?' he said. 'They went for me. Tried to peck my eyes.' He stood by the window, peering into the darkness, and could see nothing. His wife, heavy with sleep, murmured from the bed.

'I'm not making it up,' he said, angry at her suggestion. 'I tell you the birds were on the sill, trying to get into the room.'

Suddenly a frightened cry came from the room across the passage where the children slept.

'It's Jill,' said his wife, roused at the sound, sitting up in bed. 'Go to her, see what's the matter.'

Nat lit the candle, but when he opened the bedroom door to cross the passage the draught blew out the flame.

There came a second cry of terror, this time from both children, and stumbling into their room he felt the beating of wings about him in the darkness. The window was wide open. Through it came the birds, hitting first the ceiling and the walls, then swerving in mid-flight, turning to the children in their beds.

'It's all right, I'm here,' shouted Nat, and the children flung themselves, screaming, upon him, while in the darkness the birds rose and dived and came for him again.

'What is it, Nat, what's happened?' his wife called from the further bedroom, and swiftly he pushed the children through the door to the passage and shut it upon them, so that he was alone now, in their bedroom, with the birds.

He seized a blanket from the nearest bed, and using it as a weapon flung it to right and left about him in the air. He felt the thud of bodies, heard the fluttering of wings, but they were not yet defeated, for again and again they returned to the assault, jabbing his hands, his head, the little stabbing beaks sharp as a pointed fork. The blanket became a weapon of defence; he wound it about his head, and then in greater darkness beat at the birds with his bare hands. He dared not stumble to the door and open it, lest in doing so the birds should follow him.

How long he fought with them in the darkness he could not tell, but at last the beating of the wings about him lessened and then withdrew, and through the density of the blanket he was aware of light. He waited, listened; there was no sound except the fretful crying of one of the children from the bedroom beyond. The fluttering, the whirring of the wings had ceased.

He took the blanket from his head and stared about him. The cold grey morning light exposed the room. Dawn, and the open window, had called the living birds; the dead lay on the floor. Nat gazed at the little corpses, shocked and horrified. They were all small birds, none of any size; there must have been fifty of them lying there upon the floor. There were robins, finches, sparrows, blue tits, larks and bramblings, birds that by nature's law kept to their own flock and their own territory, and now, joining one with another in their urge for battle, had destroyed themselves against the bedroom walls, or in the strife had been destroyed by him. Some had lost feathers in the fight, others had blood, his blood, upon their beaks.

Sickened, Nat went to the window and stared out across his patch of garden to the fields.

It was bitter cold, and the ground had all the hard black look of frost. Not white frost, to shine in the morning sun, but the black frost that the east wind brings. The sea, fiercer now with the turning tide, white-capped and steep, broke harshly in the bay. Of the birds there was no sign. Not a sparrow chattered in the hedge beyond the garden gate, no early missel-thrush or blackbird pecked on the grass for worms. There was no sound at all but the east wind and the sea.

Nat shut the window and the door of the small bedroom, and went back across the passage to his own. His wife sat up in bed, one child asleep beside her, the smaller in her arms, his face bandaged. The curtains were tightly drawn across the window, the candles lit. Her face looked garish in the yellow light. She shook her head for silence.

'He's sleeping now,' she whispered, 'but only just. Something must have cut him, there was blood at the corner of his eyes. Jill said it was the birds. She said she woke up, and the birds were in the room.'

His wife looked up at Nat, searching his face for confirmation. She looked terrified, bewildered, and he did not want her to know that he was also shaken, dazed almost, by the events of the past few hours.

'There are birds in there,' he said, 'dead birds, nearly fifty of them. Robins, wrens, all the little birds from hereabouts. It's as though a madness seized them, with the east wind.' He sat down on the bed beside his wife, and held her hand. 'It's the weather,' he said, 'it must be that, it's the hard weather. They aren't the birds, maybe, from here around. They've been driven down, from up country.'

'But Nat,' whispered his wife, 'it's only this night that the weather turned. There's been no snow to drive them. And they can't be hungry yet. There's food for them, out there, in the fields.'

'It's the weather,' repeated Nat. 'I tell you, it's the weather.'

His face too was drawn and tired, like hers. They stared at one another for a while without speaking.

'I'll go downstairs and make a cup of tea,' he said.

The sight of the kitchen reassured him. The cups and saucers, neatly stacked upon the dresser, the table and chairs, his wife's roll of knitting on her basket chair, the children's toys in a corner cupboard.

He knelt down, raked out the old embers and relit the fire.

13

The glowing sticks brought normality, the steaming kettle and the brown teapot comfort and security. He drank his tea, carried a cup up to his wife. Then he washed in the scullery, and, putting on his boots, opened the back door.

The sky was hard and leaden, and the brown hills that had gleamed in the sun the day before looked dark and bare. The east wind, like a razor, stripped the trees, and the leaves, crackling and dry, shivered and scattered with the wind's blast. Nat stubbed the earth with his boot. It was frozen hard. He had never known a change so swift and sudden. Black winter had descended in a single night.

The children were awake now. Jill was chattering upstairs and young Johnny crying once again. Nat heard his wife's voice, soothing, comforting. Presently they came down. He had breakfast ready for them, and the routine of the day began.

'Did you drive away the birds?' asked Jill, restored to calm because of the kitchen fire, because of day, because of breakfast.

'Yes, they've all gone now,' said Nat. 'It was the east wind brought them in. They were frightened and lost, they wanted shelter.'

'They tried to peck us,' said Jill. 'They went for Johnny's eyes.'

'Fright made them do that,' said Nat. 'They didn't know where they were, in the dark bedroom.'

'I hope they won't come again,' said Jill. 'Perhaps if we put bread for them outside the window they will eat that and fly away.'

She finished her breakfast and went for her coat and hood, her school books and her satchel. Nat said nothing, but his wife looked at him across the table. A silent message passed between them.

'I'll walk with her to the bus,' he said, 'I don't go to the farm today.'

And while the child was washing in the scullery he said to his wife, 'Keep all the windows closed, and the doors too. Just to be on the safe side. I'll go to the farm. Find out if they heard anything in the night.' Then he walked with his small daughter up the lane. She seemed to have forgotten her experience of the night before. She danced ahead of him, chasing the leaves, her face whipped with the cold and rosy under the pixie hood.

'Is it going to snow, Dad?' she said. 'It's cold enough.'

He glanced up at the bleak sky, felt the wind tear at his shoulders.

'No,' he said, 'it's not going to snow. This is a black winter, not a white one.'

All the while he searched the hedgerows for the birds, glanced over the top of them to the fields beyond, looked to the small wood above the farm where the rooks and jackdaws gathered. He saw none.

The other children waited by the bus-stop, muffled, hooded like Jill, the faces white and pinched with cold.

Jill ran to them, waving. 'My Dad says it won't snow,' she called, 'it's going to be a black winter.'

She said nothing of the birds. She began to push and struggle with another little girl. The bus came ambling up the hill. Nat saw her onto it, then turned and walked back towards the farm. It was not his day for work, but he wanted to satisfy himself that all was well. Jim, the cowman, was clattering in the yard.

'Boss around?' asked Nat.

'Gone to market,' said Jim. 'It's Tuesday, isn't it?'

He clumped off round the corner of a shed. He had no time for Nat. Nat was said to be superior. Read books, and the like. Nat had forgotten it was Tuesday. This showed how the events of the preceding night had shaken him. He went to the back door of the farm-house and heard Mrs Trigg singing in the kitchen, the wireless making a background to her song.

'Are you there, missus?' called out Nat.

She came to the door, beaming, broad, a good-tempered woman.

'Hullo, Mr Hocken,' she said. 'Can you tell me where this

cold is coming from? Is it Russia? I've never seen such a change. And it's going on, the wireless says. Something to do with the Arctic circle.'

'We didn't turn on the wireless this morning,' said Nat. 'Fact is, we had trouble in the night.'

'Kiddies poorly?'

'No ...' He hardly knew how to explain it. Now, in daylight, the battle of the birds would sound absurd.

He tried to tell Mrs Trigg what had happened, but he could see from her eyes that she thought his story was the result of a nightmare.

'Sure they were real birds,' she said, smiling, 'with proper feathers and all? Not the funny-shaped kind, that the men see after closing hours on a Saturday night?'

'Mrs Trigg,' he said, 'there are fifty dead birds, robins, wrens, and such, lying low on the floor of the children's bedroom. They went for me, they tried to go for young Johnny's eyes.'

Mrs Trigg stared at him doubtfully.

'Well there, now,' she answered, 'I suppose the weather brought them. Once in the bedroom, they wouldn't know where they were to. Foreign birds maybe, from that Arctic circle.'

'No,' said Nat, 'they were the birds you see about here every day.'

'Funny thing,' said Mrs Trigg, 'no explaining it really. You ought to write up and ask the *Guardian*. They'd have some answer for it. Well, I must be getting on.'

She nodded, smiled, and went back into the kitchen.

Nat, dissatisfied, turned to the farm-gate. Had it not been for these corpses on the bedroom floor, which he must now collect and bury somewhere, he would have considered the tale exaggeration too.

Jim was standing by the gate.

'Had any trouble with the birds?' asked Nat.

'Birds? What birds?'

'We got them up our place last night. Scores of them, came

in the children's bedroom. Quite savage they were.'

'Oh?' It took time for anything to penetrate Jim's head. 'Never heard of birds acting savage,' he said at length. 'They get tame, like, sometimes. I've seen them come to the windows for crumbs.'

'These birds last night weren't tame.'

'No? Cold maybe. Hungry. You put out some crumbs.'

Jim was no more interested than Mrs Trigg had been. It was, Nat thought, like air-raids in the war. No one down this end of the country knew what the Plymouth folk had seen and suffered. You had to endure something yourself before it touched you. He walked back along the lane and crossed the stile to his cottage. He found his wife in the kitchen with young Johnny.

'See anyone?' she asked.

'Mrs Trigg and Jim,' he answered. 'I don't think they believed me. Anyway, nothing wrong up there.'

'You might take the birds away,' she said. 'I daren't go into the room to make the beds until you do. I'm scared.'

'Nothing to scare you now,' said Nat. 'They're dead, aren't they?'

He went up with a sack and dropped the stiff bodies into it, one by one. Yes, there were fifty of them, all told. Just the ordinary common birds of the hedgerow, nothing as large even as a thrush. It must have been fright that made them act the way they did. Blue tits, wrens, it was incredible to think of the power of their small beaks, jabbing at his face and hands the night before. He took the sack out into the garden and was faced now with a fresh problem. The ground was too hard to dig. It was frozen solid, yet no snow had fallen, nothing had happened in the past hours but the coming of the east wind. It was unnatural, queer. The weather prophets must be right. The change was something connected with the Arctic circle.

The wind seemed to cut him to the bone as he stood there, uncertainly, holding the sack. He could see the white-capped seas breaking down under in the bay. He decided to take the birds to the shore and bury them.

When he reached the beach below the headland he could scarcely stand, the force of the east wind was so strong. It hurt to draw breath, and his bare hands were blue. Never had he known such cold, not in all the bad winters he could remember. It was low tide. He crunched his way over the shingle to the softer sand and then, his back to the wind, ground a pit in the sand with his heel. He meant to drop the birds into it, but as he opened up the sack the force of the wind carried them, lifted them, as though in flight again, and they were blown away from him along the beach, tossed like feathers, spread and scattered, the bodies of the fifty frozen birds. There was something ugly in the sight. He did not like it. The dead birds were swept away from him by the wind.

'The tide will take them when it turns,' he said to himself.

He looked out to sea and watched the crested breakers, combing green. They rose stiffly, curled, and broke again, and because it was ebb tide the roar was distant, more remote, lacking the sound and thunder of the flood.

Then he saw them. The gulls. Out there, riding the seas.

What he had thought at first to be the white caps of the waves were gulls. Hundreds, thousands, tens of thousands ... They rose and fell in the trough of the seas, heads to the wind, like a mighty fleet at anchor, waiting on the tide. To eastward, and to the west, the gulls were there. They stretched as far as his eye could reach, in close formation, line upon line. Had the sea been still they would have covered the bay like a white cloud, head to head, body packed to body. Only the east wind, whipping the sea to breakers, hid them from the shore.

Nat turned, and leaving the beach climbed the steep path home. Someone should know of this. Someone should be told. Something was happening, because of the east wind and the weather, that he did not understand. He wondered if he should go to the call-box by the bus-stop and ring up the police. Yet what could they do? What could anyone do? Tens and thousands of gulls riding the sea there, in the bay, because of storm, because of hunger. The police would think him mad, or drunk, or take the statement from him with great calm. 'Thank you. Yes, the matter has already been reported. The hard weather is driving the birds inland in great numbers.' Nat looked about him. Still no sign of any other bird. Perhaps the cold had sent them all from up country? As he drew near to the cottage his wife came to meet him, at the door. She called to him, excited. 'Nat,' she said, 'it's on the wireless. They've just read out a special news bulletin. I've written it down.'

'What's on the wireless?' he said.

'About the birds,' she said. 'It's not only here, it's everywhere. In London, all over the country. Something has happened to the birds.'

Together they went into the kitchen. He read the piece of paper lying on the table.

'Statement from the Home Office at eleven a.m. today. Reports from all over the country are coming in hourly about the vast quantity of birds flocking above towns, villages, and outlying districts, causing obstruction and damage and even attacking individuals. It is thought that the Arctic air stream, at present covering the British Isles, is causing birds to migrate south in immense numbers, and that intense hunger may drive these birds to attack human beings. Householders are warned to see to their windows, doors, and chimneys, and to take reasonable precautions for the safety of their children. A further statement will be issued later.'

A kind of excitement seized Nat; he looked at his wife in triumph.

'There you are,' he said, 'let's hope they'll hear that at the farm. Mrs Trigg will know it wasn't any story. It's true. All over the country. I've been telling myself all morning there's something wrong. And just now, down on the beach. I looked out to sea and there are gulls, thousands of them, tens of thousands, you couldn't put a pin between their heads, and they're all out there, riding on the sea, waiting.'

'What are they waiting for, Nat?' she asked.

He stared at her, then looked down again at the piece of

paper. 'I don't know,' he said slowly. 'It says here the birds are hungry.'

He went over to the drawer where he kept his hammer and tools.

'What are you going to do, Nat?'

'See to the windows and the chimneys too, like they tell you.'

'You think they would break in, with the windows shut? Those sparrows and robins and such? Why, how could they?'

He did not answer. He was not thinking of the robins and the sparrows. He was thinking of the gulls....

He went upstairs and worked there the rest of the morning, boarding the windows of the bedrooms, filling up the chimney bases. Good job it was his free day and he was not working at the farm. It reminded him of the old days, at the beginning of the war. He was not married then, and he had made all the blackout boards for his mother's house in Plymouth. Made the shelter too. Not that it had been of any use, when the moment came. He wondered if they would take these precautions up at the farm. He doubted it. Too easygoing, Harry Trigg and his missus. Maybe they'd laugh at the whole thing. Go off to a dance or a whist drive.

'Dinner's ready.' She called him, from the kitchen.

'All right. Coming down.'

He was pleased with his handiwork. The frames fitted nicely over the little panes and at the base of the chimneys.

When dinner was over and his wife was washing up, Nat switched on the one o'clock news. The same announcement was repeated, the one which she had taken down during the morning, but the news bulletin enlarged upon it. 'The flocks of birds have caused dislocation in all areas,' read the announcer, 'and in London the sky was so dense at ten o'clock this morning that it seemed as if the city was covered by a vast black cloud.

'The birds settled on roof-tops, on window ledges and on chimneys. The species included blackbird, thrush, the common house-sparrow, and, as might be expected in the metropolis, a vast quantity of pigeons and starlings, and that frequenter of the London river, the black-headed gull. The sight has been so unusual that traffic came to a standstill in many thoroughfares, work was abandoned in shops and offices, and the streets and pavements were crowded with people standing about to watch the birds.'

Various incidents were recounted, the suspected reason of cold and hunger stated again, and warnings to householders repeated. The announcer's voice was smooth and suave. Nat had the impression that this man, in particular, treated the whole business as he would an elaborate joke. There would be others like him, hundreds of them who did not know what it was to struggle in darkness with a flock of birds. There would be parties tonight in London, like the ones they gave on election nights. People standing about, shouting and laughing, getting drunk. 'Come and watch the birds!'

Nat switched off the wireless. He got up and started work on the kitchen windows. His wife watched him, young Johnny at her heels.

'What, boards for down here too?' she said. 'Why, I'll have to light up before three o'clock. I see no call for boards down here.'

'Better be sure than sorry,' answered Nat. 'I'm not going to take any chances.'

'What they ought to do,' she said, 'is to call the army out and shoot the birds. That would soon scare them off.'

'Let them try,' said Nat. 'How'd they set about it?'

'They have the army to the docks,' she answered, 'when the dockers strike. The soldiers go down and unload the ships.'

'Yes,' said Nat, 'and the population of London is eight million or more. Think of all the buildings, all the flats, and houses. Do you think they've enough soldiers to go round shooting birds from every roof?'

'I don't know. But something should be done. They ought to do something.'

Nat thought to himself that 'they' were no doubt

considering the problem at that very moment, but whatever 'they' decided to do in London and the big cities would not help the people here, three hundred miles away. Each householder must look after his own.

'How are we off for food?' he said.

'Now, Nat, whatever next?'

'Never mind. What have you got in the larder?'

'It's shopping day tomorrow, you know that. I don't keep uncooked food hanging about, it goes off. Butcher doesn't call till the day after. But I can bring back something when I go in tomorrow.'

Nat did not want to scare her. He thought it possible that she might not go to town tomorrow. He looked in the larder for himself, and in the cupboard where she kept her tins. They would do, for a couple of days. Bread was low.

'What about the baker?'

'He comes tomorrow too.'

He saw she had flour. If the baker did not call she had enough to bake one loaf.

'We'd be better off in the old days,' he said, 'when the women baked twice a week, and had pilchards salted, and there was food for a family to last a siege, if need be.'

'I've tried the children with tinned fish, they don't like it,' she said.

Nat went on hammering the boards across the kitchen windows. Candles. They were low in candles too. That must be another thing she meant to buy tomorrow. Well, it could not be helped. They must go early to bed tonight. That was, if ...

He got up and went out of the back door and stood in the garden, looking down towards the sea. There had been no sun all day, and now, at barely three o'clock, a kind of darkness had already come, the sky sullen, heavy, colourless like salt. He could hear the vicious sea drumming on the rocks. He walked down the path, half-way to the beach. And then he stopped. He could see the tide had turned. The rock that had shown in mid-morning was now covered, but it was not the sea that held his eyes. The gulls had risen. They were circling, hundreds of them, thousands of them, lifting their wings against the wind. It was the gulls that made the darkening of the sky. And they were silent. They made not a sound. They just went on soaring and circling, rising, falling, trying their strength against the wind.

Nat turned. He ran up the path, back to the cottage.

'I'm going for Jill,' he said. 'I'll wait for her, at the bus-stop.'

'What's the matter?' asked his wife. 'You've gone quite white.'

'Keep Johnny inside,' he said. 'Keep the door shut. Light up now, and draw the curtains.'

'It's only just gone three,' she said.

'Never mind. Do what I tell you.'

He looked inside the toolshed, outside the back door. Nothing there of much use. A spade was too heavy, and a fork no good. He took the hoe. It was the only possible tool, and light enough to carry.

He started walking up the lane to the bus-stop, and now and again glanced back over his shoulder.

The gulls had risen higher now, their circles were broader, wider, they were spreading out in huge formation across the sky.

He hurried on; although he knew the bus would not come to the top of the hill before four o'clock he had to hurry. He passed no one on the way. He was glad of this. No time to stop and chatter.

At the top of the hill he waited. He was much too soon. There was half an hour still to go. The east wind came whipping across the fields from the higher ground. He stamped his feet and blew upon his hands. In the distance he could see the clay hills, white and clean, against the heavy pallor of the sky. Something black rose from behind them, like a smudge at first, then widening, becoming deeper, and the smudge became a cloud, and the cloud divided again into five other clouds, spreading north, east, south and west, and

23

they were not clouds at all; they were birds. He watched them travel across the sky, and as one section passed overhead, within two or three hundred feet of him, he knew, from their speed, they were bound inland, up country, they had no business with people here on the peninsula. They were rooks, crows, jackdaws, magpies, jays, all birds that usually preyed upon the smaller species; but this afternoon they were bound on some other mission.

'They've been given the towns,' thought Nat, 'they know what they have to do. We don't matter so much here. The gulls will serve for us. The others go to the towns.'

He went to the call-box, stepped inside and lifted the receiver. The exchange would do. They would pass the message on.

'I'm speaking from Highway,' he said, 'by the bus-stop. I want to report large formations of birds travelling up country. The gulls are also forming in the bay.'

'All right,' answered the voice, laconic, weary.

'You'll be sure and pass this message onto the proper quarter?'

'Yes ... yes ...' Impatient now, fed-up. The buzzing note resumed.

'She's another,' thought Nat, 'she doesn't care. Maybe she's had to answer calls all day. She hopes to go to the pictures tonight. She'll squeeze some fellow's hand, and point up at the sky, and "Look at all them birds!" She doesn't care.'

The bus came lumbering up the hill, Jill climbed out and three or four other children. The bus went on towards the town.

'What's the hoe for, Dad?'

They crowded around him, laughing, pointing.

'I just brought it along,' he said. 'Come on now, let's get home. It's cold, no hanging about. Here, you. I'll watch you across the fields, see how fast you can run.'

He was speaking to Jill's companions who came from different families, living in the council houses. A short cut would take them to the cottages.

'We want to play a bit in the lane,' said one of them.

'No, you don't. You go off home, or I'll tell your mammy.'

They whispered to one another, round-eyed, then scuttled off across the fields. Jill stared at her father, her mouth sullen.

'We always play in the lane,' she said.

'Not tonight, you don't,' he said. 'Come on now, no dawdling.'

He could see the gulls now, circling the fields, coming in towards the land. Still silent. Still no sound.

'Look, Dad, look over there, look at the gulls.'

'Yes. Hurry, now.'

'Where are they flying to? Where are they going?'

'Up country, I dare say. Where it's warmer.'

He seized her hand and dragged her after him along the lane.

'Don't go so fast. I can't keep up.'

The gulls were copying the rooks and crows. They were spreading out in formation across the sky. They headed, in bands of thousands, to the four compass points.

'Dad, what is it? What are the gulls doing?'

They were not intent upon their flight, as the crows, as the jackdaws had been. They still circled overhead. Nor did they fly so high. It was as though they waited upon some signal. As though some decision had yet to be given. The order was not clear.

'Do you want me to carry you, Jill? Here, come pick-a-back.'

This way he might put on speed; but he was wrong. Jill was heavy. She kept slipping. And she was crying too. His sense of urgency, of fear, had communicated itself to the child.

'I wish the gulls would go away. I don't like them. They're coming closer to the lane.'

He put her down again. He started running, swinging Jill after him. As they went past the farm turning he saw the farmer backing his car out of the garage. Nat called to him.

'Can you give us a lift?' he said.

'What's that?'

Mr Trigg turned in the driving seat and stared at them. Then a smile came to his cheerful, rubicund face.

'It looks as though we're in for some fun,' he said. 'Have you seen the gulls? Jim and I are going to take a crack at them. Everyone's gone bird crazy, talking of nothing else. I hear you were troubled in the night. Want a gun?'

Nat shook his head.

The small car was packed. There was just room for Jill, if she crouched on top of petrol tins on the back seat.

'I don't want a gun,' said Nat, 'but I'd be obliged if you'd run Jill home. She's scared of the birds.'

He spoke briefly. He did not want to talk in front of Jill.

'OK,' said the farmer, 'I'll take her home. Why don't you stop behind and join the shooting match? We'll make the feathers fly.'

Jill climbed in, and turning the car the driver sped up the lane. Nat followed after. Trigg must be crazy. What use was a gun against a sky of birds?

Now Nat was not responsible for Jill he had time to look about him. The birds were circling still, above the fields. Mostly herring gull, but the black-backed gull amongst them. Usually they kept apart. Now they were united. Some bond had brought them together. It was the black-backed gull that attacked the smaller birds, and even new-born lambs, so he'd heard. He'd never seen it done. He remembered this now, though, looking above him in the sky. They were coming in towards the farm. They were circling lower in the sky, and the black-backed gulls were to the front, the black-backed gulls were leading. The farm, then, was their target. They were making for the farm.

Nat increased his pace towards his own cottage. He saw the farmer's car turn and come back along the lane. It drew up beside him with a jerk.

'The kid has run inside,' said the farmer. 'Your wife was watching for her. Well, what do you make of it? They're saying in town the Russians have done it. The Russians have poisoned the birds.'

'How could they do that?' asked Nat.

'Don't ask me. You know how stories get around. Will you join my shooting match?'

'No, I'll get along home. The wife will be worried else.'

'My missus says if you could eat gull, there'd be some sense in it,' said Trigg, 'we'd have roast gull, baked gull, and pickle 'em into the bargain. You wait until I let off a few barrels into the brutes. That'll scare 'em.'

'Have you boarded your windows?' asked Nat.

'No. Lot of nonsense. They like to scare you on the wireless I've had more to do today than to go round boarding up my windows.'

'I'd board them now, if I were you.'

'Garn. You're windy. Like to come to our place to sleep?'

'No, thanks all the same.'

'All right. See you in the morning. Give you a gull breakfast.'

The farmer grinned and turned his car to the farm entrance.

Nat hurried on. Past the little wood, past the old barn, and then across the stile to the remaining field.

As he jumped the stile he heard the whirr of wings. A black-backed gull dived down at him from the sky, missed, swerved in flight, and rose to dive again. In a moment it was joined by others, six, seven, a dozen, black-backed and herring mixed. Nat dropped his hoe. The hoe was useless. Covering his head with his arms he ran towards the cottage. They kept coming at him from the air, silent save for the beating wings. The terrible, fluttering wings. He could feel the blood on his hands, his wrists, his neck. Each stab of a swooping beak tore his flesh. If only he could keep them from his eyes. Nothing else mattered. He must keep them from his eyes. They had not learnt yet how to cling to a shoulder, how to rip clothing, how to dive in mass upon the head, upon the body. But with each dive, with each attack, they became

27

bolder. And they had no thought for themselves. When they dived low and missed, they crashed, bruised and broken, on the ground. As Nat ran he stumbled, kicking their spent bodies in front of him.

He found the door, he hammered upon it with his bleeding hands. Because of the boarded windows no light shone. Everything was dark.

'Let me in,' he shouted, 'it's Nat. Let me in.'

He shouted loud to make himself heard above the whirr of the gulls' wings.

Then he saw the gannet, poised for the dive, above him in the sky. The gulls circled, retired, soared, one with another, against the wind. Only the gannet remained. One single gannet, above him in the sky. The wings folded suddenly to its body. It dropped, like a stone. Nat screamed, and the door opened. He stumbled across the threshold, and his wife threw her weight against the door.

They heard the thud of the gannet as it fell.

His wife dressed his wounds. They were not deep. The backs of his hands had suffered most, and his wrists. Had he not worn a cap they would have reached his head. As to the gannet ... the gannet could have split his skull.

The children were crying, of course. They had seen the blood on their father's hands.

'It's all right now,' he told them. 'I'm not hurt. Just a few scratches. You play with Johnny, Jill. Mammy will wash these cuts.'

He half shut the door to the scullery, so that they could not see. His wife was ashen. She began running water from the sink.

'I saw them overhead,' she whispered. 'They began collecting just as Jill ran in with Mr Trigg. I shut the door fast, and it jammed. That's why I couldn't open it at once, when you came.'

'Thank God they waited for me,' he said. 'Jill would have fallen at once. One bird alone would have done it.'

Furtively, so as not to alarm the children, they whispered together, as she bandaged his hands and the back of his neck.

'They're flying inland,' he said, 'thousands of them. Rooks, crows, all the bigger birds. I saw them from the bus-stop. They're making for the towns.'

'But what can they do, Nat?'

'They'll attack. Go for everyone out in the streets. Then they'll try the windows, the chimneys.'

'Why don't the authorities do something? Why don't they get the army, get machine-guns, anything?'

'There's been no time. Nobody's prepared. We'll hear what they have to say on the six o'clock news.'

Nat went back into the kitchen, followed by his wife. Johnny was playing quietly on the floor. Only Jill looked anxious.

'I can hear the birds,' she said. 'Listen, Dad.'

Nat listened. Muffled sounds came from the windows, from the door. Wings brushing the surface, sliding, scraping, seeking a way of entry. The sound of many bodies, pressed together, shuffling on the sills. Now and again came a thud, a crash, as some bird dived and fell. 'Some of them will kill themselves that way,' he thought, 'but not enough. Never enough.'

'All right,' he said aloud, 'I've got boards over the windows, Jill. The birds can't get in.'

He went and examined all the windows. His work had been thorough. Every gap was closed. He would make extra certain, however. He found wedges, pieces of old tin, strips of wood and metal, and fastened them at the sides to reinforce the boards. His hammering helped to deafen the sound of the birds, the shuffling, the tapping, and more ominous – he did not want his wife or the children to hear it – the splinter of cracked glass.

'Turn on the wireless,' he said, 'let's have the wireless.'

This would drown the sound also. He went upstairs to the bedrooms and reinforced the windows there. Now he could hear the birds on the roof, the scraping of claws, a sliding, jostling sound.

He decided they must sleep in the kitchen, keep up the fire, bring down the mattresses and lay them out on the floor. He was afraid of the bedroom chimneys. The boards he had placed at the chimney bases might give way. In the kitchen they would be safe, because of the fire. He would have to make a joke of it. Pretend to the children they were playing at camp. If the worst happened, and the birds forced an entry down the bedroom chimneys, it would be hours, days perhaps, before they could break down the doors. The birds would be imprisoned in the bedrooms. They could do no harm there. Crowded together, they would stifle and die.

He began to bring the mattresses downstairs. At sight of them his wife's eyes widened in apprehension. She thought the birds had already broken in upstairs.

'All right,' he said cheerfully, 'we'll all sleep together in the kitchen tonight. More cosy here by the fire. Then we shan't be worried by those silly old birds tapping at the windows.'

He made the children help him rearrange the furniture, and he took the precaution of moving the dresser, with his wife's help, across the window. It fitted well. It was an added safeguard. The mattresses could now be lain, one beside the other, against the wall where the dresser had stood.

'We're safe enough now,' he thought, 'we're snug and tight, like an air-raid shelter. We can hold out. It's just the food that worries me. Food, and coal for the fire. We've enough for two or three days, not more. By that time ...'

No use thinking ahead as far as that. And they'd be giving directions on the wireless. People would be told what to do. And now, in the midst of many problems, he realised that it was dance music only coming over the air. Not Children's Hour, as it should have been. He glanced at the dial. Yes, they were on the Home Service all right. Dance records. He switched to the Light programme. He knew the reason. The usual programmes had been abandoned. This only happened at exceptional times. Elections, and such. He tried to remember if it had happened in the war, during the heavy raids on London. But of course. The BBC was not stationed in

London during the war. The programmes were broadcast from other, temporary quarters. 'We're better off here,' he thought, 'we're better off here in the kitchen, with the windows and the doors boarded, than they are up in the towns. Thank God we're not in the towns.'

At six o'clock the records ceased. The time signal was given. No matter if it scared the children, he must hear the news. There was a pause after the pips. Then the announcer spoke. His voice was solemn, grave. Quite different from midday.

'This is London,' he said. 'A National Emergency was proclaimed at four o'clock this afternoon. Measures are being taken to safeguard the lives and property of the population, but it must be understood that these are not easy to effect immediately, owing to the unforeseen and unparalleled nature of the present crisis. Every householder must take precautions to his own building, and where several people live together, as in flats and apartments, they must unite to do the utmost they can to prevent entry. It is absolutely imperative that every individual stays indoors tonight, and that no one at all remains on the streets, or roads, or anywhere without doors. The birds, in vast numbers, are attacking anyone on sight, and have already begun an assault upon buildings; but these, with due care, should be impenetrable. The population is asked to remain calm, and not to panic. Owing to the exceptional nature of the emergency, there will be no further transmission from any broadcasting station until seven a.m. tomorrow.'

They played the National Anthem. Nothing more happened. Nat switched off the set. He looked at his wife. She stared back at him.

'What's it mean?' said Jill. 'What did the news say?'

'There won't be any more programmes tonight,' said Nat. 'There's been a breakdown at the BBC.'

'Is it the birds?' asked Jill. 'Have the birds done it?'

'No,' said Nat, 'it's just that everyone's very busy, and then of course they have to get rid of the birds, messing everything up, in the towns. Well, we can manage without the wireless for one evening.'

'I wish we had a gramophone,' said Jill, 'that would be better than nothing.'

She had her face turned to the dresser, backed against the windows. Try as they did to ignore it, they were all aware of the shuffling, the stabbing, the persistent beating and sweeping of wings.

'We'll have supper early,' suggested Nat, 'something for a treat. Ask Mammy. Toasted cheese, eh? Something we all like?'

He winked and nodded at his wife. He wanted the look of dread, of apprehension, to go from Jill's face.

He helped with the supper, whistling, singing, making as much clatter as he could, and it seemed to him that the shuffling and the tapping were not so intense as they had been at first. Presently he went up to the bedrooms and listened, and he no longer heard the jostling for place upon the roof.

'They've got reasoning powers,' he thought, 'they know it's hard to break in here. They'll try elsewhere. They won't waste their time with us.'

Supper passed without incident, and then, when they were clearing away, they heard a new sound, droning, familiar, a sound they all knew and understood.

His wife looked up at him, her face alight. 'It's planes,' she said, 'they're sending out planes after the birds. That's what I said they ought to do, all along. That will get them. Isn't that gun-fire? Can't you hear guns?'

It might be gun-fire, out at sea. Nat could not tell. Big naval guns might have an effect upon the gulls out at sea, but the gulls were inland now. The guns couldn't shell the shore, because of the population.

'It's good, isn't it,' said his wife, 'to hear the planes?'

And Jill, catching her enthusiasm, jumped up and down with Johnny. 'The planes will get the birds. The planes will shoot them.'

Just then they heard a crash about two miles distant,

followed by a second, then a third. The droning became more distant, passed away out to sea.

'What was that?' asked his wife. 'Were they dropping bombs on the birds?'

'I don't know,' answered Nat, 'I don't think so.'

He did not want to tell her that the sound they had heard was the crashing of aircraft. It was, he had no doubt, a venture on the part of the authorities to send out reconnaissance forces, but they might have known the venture was suicidal. What could aircraft do against birds that flung themselves to death against propeller and fuselage, but hurtle to the ground themselves? This was being tried now, he supposed, over the whole country. And at a cost. Someone high up had lost his head.

'Where have the planes gone, Dad?' asked Jill.

'Back to base,' he said. 'Come on, now, time to tuck down for bed.'

It kept his wife occupied, undressing the children before the fire, seeing to the bedding, one thing and another, while he went round the cottage again, making sure that nothing had worked loose. There was no further drone of aircraft, and the naval guns had ceased. 'Waste of life and effort,' Nat said to himself. 'We can't destroy enough of them that way. Cost too heavy. There's always gas. Maybe they'll try spraying with gas, mustard gas. We'll be warned first, of course, if they do. There's one thing, the best brains of the country will be on to it tonight.'

Somehow the thought reassured him. He had a picture of scientists, naturalists, technicians, and all those chaps they called the back-room boys, summoned to a council; they'd be working on the problem now. This was not a job for the government, for the chiefs-of-staff – they would merely carry out the orders of the scientists.

'They'll have to be ruthless,' he thought. 'Where the trouble's worst they'll have to risk more lives, if they use gas. All the livestock, too, and the soil – all contaminated. As long as everyone doesn't panic. That's the trouble. People panicking, losing their heads. The BBC was right to warn us of that.'

Upstairs in the bedrooms all was quiet. No further scraping and stabbing at the windows. A lull in battle. Forces regrouping. Wasn't that what they called it, in the old war-time bulletins? The wind hadn't dropped, though. He could still hear it, roaring in the chimneys. And the sea breaking down on the shore. Then he remembered the tide. The tide would be on the turn. Maybe the lull in battle was because of the tide. There was some law the birds obeyed, and it was all to do with the east wind and the tide.

He glanced at his watch. Nearly eight o'clock. It must have gone high water an hour ago. That explained the lull: the birds attacked with the flood tide. It might not work that way inland, up country, but it seemed as if it was so this way on the coast. He reckoned the time limit in his head. They had six hours to go, without attack. When the tide turned again, around one-twenty in the morning, the birds would come back....

There were two things he could do. The first to rest, with his wife and the children, and all of them snatch what sleep they could, until the small hours. The second to go out, see how they were faring at the farm, see if the telephone was still working there, so that they might get news from the exchange.

He called softly to his wife, who had just settled the children. She came half-way up the stairs and he whispered to her.

'You're not to go,' she said at once, 'you're not to go and leave me alone with the children. I can't stand it.'

Her voice rose hysterically. He hushed her, calmed her.

'All right,' he said, 'all right. I'll wait till morning. And we'll get the wireless bulletin then too, at seven. But in the morning, when the tide ebbs again, I'll try for the farm, and they may let us have bread and potatoes, and milk too.'

His mind was busy again, planning against emergency. They would not have milked, of course, this evening. The cows would be standing by the gate, waiting in the yard, with the household inside, battened behind boards, as they were here at the cottage. That is, if they had time to take precautions. He thought of the farmer, Trigg, smiling at him from the car. There would have been no shooting party, not tonight.

The children were asleep. His wife, still clothed, was sitting on her mattress. She watched him, her eyes nervous.

'What are you going to do?' she whispered.

He shook his head for silence. Softly, stealthily, he opened the back door and looked outside.

It was pitch dark. The wind was blowing harder than ever, coming in steady gusts, icy, from the sea. He kicked at the step outside the door. It was heaped with birds. There were dead birds everywhere. Under the windows, against the walls. These were the suicides, the divers, the ones with broken necks. Wherever he looked he saw dead birds. No trace of the living. The living had flown seaward with the turn of the tide. The gulls would be riding the seas now, as they had done in the forenoon.

In the far distance, on the hill where the tractor had been two days before, something was burning. One of the aircraft that had crashed; the fire, fanned by the wind, had set light to a stack.

He looked at the bodies of the birds, and he had a notion that if he heaped them, one upon the other, on the window sills they would make added protection for the next attack. Not much, perhaps, but something. The bodies would have to be clawed at, pecked, and dragged aside, before the living birds gained purchase on the sills and attacked the panes. He set to work in the darkness. It was queer; he hated touching them. The bodies were still warm and bloody. The blood matted their feathers. He felt his stomach turn, but he went on with his work. He noticed, grimly, that every window-pane was shattered. Only the boards had kept the birds from breaking in. He stuffed the cracked panes with the bleeding bodies of the birds.

When he had finished he went back into the cottage. He barricaded the kitchen door, made it doubly secure. He took off his bandages, sticky with the birds' blood, not with his own cuts, and put on fresh plaster.

His wife had made him cocoa and he drank it thirstily. He was very tired.

'All right,' he said, smiling, 'don't worry. We'll get through.'

He lay down on his mattress and closed his eyes. He slept at once. He dreamt uneasily, because through his dreams there ran a thread of something forgotten. Some piece of work, neglected, that he should have done. Some precaution that he had known well but had not taken, and he could not put a name to it in his dreams. It was connected in some way with the burning aircraft and the stack upon the hill. He went on sleeping, though; he did not awake. It was his wife shaking his shoulder that awoke him finally.

'They've begun,' she sobbed, 'they've started this last hour, I can't listen to it any longer, alone. There's something smelling bad too, something burning.'

Then he remembered. He had forgotten to make up the fire. It was smouldering, nearly out. He got up swiftly and lit the lamp. The hammering had started at the windows and the doors, but it was not that he minded now. It was the smell of singed feathers. The smell filled the kitchen. He knew at once what it was. The birds were coming down the chimney, squeezing their way down to the kitchen range.

He got sticks and paper and put them on the embers, then reached for the can of paraffin.

'Stand back,' he shouted to his wife, 'we've got to risk this.'

He threw the paraffin on to the fire. The flame roared up the pipe, and down upon the fire fell the scorched, blackened bodies of the birds.

The children woke, crying. 'What is it?' said Jill. 'What's happened?'

Nat had no time to answer. He was raking the bodies from

the chimney, clawing them out onto the floor. The flames still roared, and the danger of the chimney catching fire was one he had to take. The flames would send away the living birds from the chimney top. The lower joint was the difficulty, though. This was choked with the smouldering helpless bodies of the birds caught by fire. He scarcely heeded the attack on the windows and the door: let them beat their wings, break their beaks, lose their lives, in the attempt to force an entry into his home. They would not break in. He thanked God he had one of the old cottages, with small windows, stout walls. Not like the new council houses. Heaven help them up the lane, in the new council houses.

'Stop crying,' he called to the children. 'There's nothing to be afraid of, stop crying.'

He went on raking at the burning, smouldering bodies as they fell into the fire.

'This'll fetch them,' he said to himself, 'the draught and the flames together. We're all right, as long as the chimney doesn't catch. I ought to be shot for this. It's all my fault. Last thing I should have made up the fire. I knew there was something.'

Amid the scratching and tearing at the window boards came the sudden homely striking of the kitchen clock. Three a.m. A little more than four hours yet to go. He could not be sure of the exact time of high water. He reckoned it would not turn much before half past seven, twenty to eight.

'Light up the primus,' he said to his wife. 'Make us some tea, and the kids some cocoa. No use sitting around doing nothing.'

That was the line. Keep her busy, and the children too. Move about, eat, drink; always best to be on the go.

He waited by the range. The flames were dying. But no more blackened bodies fell from the chimney. He thrust his poker up as far as it could go and found nothing. It was clear. The chimney was clear. He wiped the sweat from his forehead.

'Come on now, Jill,' he said, 'bring me some more sticks. We'll have a good fire going directly.' She wouldn't come near him, though. She was staring at the heaped singed bodies of the birds.

'Never mind them,' he said, 'we'll put those in the passage when I've got the fire steady.'

The danger of the chimney was over. It could not happen again, not if the fire was kept burning day and night.

'I'll have to get more fuel from the farm tomorrow,' he thought. 'This will never last. I'll manage, though. I can do all that with the ebb tide. It can be worked, fetching what we need, when the tide's turned. We've just got to adapt ourselves, that's all.'

They drank tea and cocoa and ate slices of bread and Bovril. Only half a loaf left, Nat noticed. Never mind though, they'd get by.

'Stop it,' said young Johnny, pointing to the windows with his spoon, 'stop it, you old birds.'

'That's right,' said Nat, smiling, 'we don't want the old beggars, do we? Had enough of 'em.'

They began to cheer when they heard the thud of the suicide birds.

'There's another, Dad,' cried Jill, 'he's done for.'

'He's had it,' said Nat, 'there he goes, the blighter.'

This was the way to face up to it. This was the spirit. If they could keep this up, hang on like this until seven, when the first news bulletin came through, they would not have done too badly.

'Give us a fag,' he said to his wife. 'A bit of smoke will clear away the smell of the scorched feathers.'

'There's only two left in the packet,' she said. 'I was going to buy you some from the Co-op.'

'I'll have one,' he said, 't'other will keep for a rainy day.'

No sense trying to make the children rest. There was no rest to be got while the tapping and the scratching went on at the windows. He sat with one arm round his wife and the other round Jill, with Johnny on his mother's lap and the blankets heaped about them on the mattress.

'You can't help admiring the beggars,' he said, 'they've got persistence. You'd think they'd tire of the game, but not a bit of it.'

Admiration was hard to sustain. The tapping went on and on and a new rasping note struck Nat's ear, as though a sharper beak than any hitherto had come to take over from its fellows. He tried to remember the names of birds, he tried to think which species would go for this particular job. It was not the tap of the woodpecker. That would be light and frequent. This was more serious, because if it continued long the wood would splinter as the glass had done. Then he remembered the hawks. Could the hawks have taken over from the gulls? Were there buzzards now upon the sills, using talons as well as beaks? Hawks, buzzards, kestrels, falcons — he had forgotten the birds of prey. He had forgotten the gripping power of the birds of prey. Three hours to go, and while they waited the sound of the splintering wood, the talons tearing at the wood.

Nat looked about him, seeing what furniture he could destroy to fortify the door. The windows were safe, because of the dresser. He was not certain of the door. He went upstairs, but when he reached the landing he paused and listened. There was a soft patter on the floor of the children's bedroom. The birds had broken through ... He put his ear to the door. No mistake. He could hear the rustle of wings, and the light patter as they searched the floor. The other bedroom was still clear. He went into it and began bringing out the furniture, to pile at the head of the stairs should the door of the children's bedroom go. It was a preparation. It might never be needed. He could not stack the furniture against the door, because it opened inward. The only possible thing was to have it at the top of the stairs.

'Come down, Nat, what are you doing?' called his wife.

'I won't be long,' he shouted. 'Just making everything shipshape up here.'

He did not want her to come; he did not want her to hear the pattering of the feet in the children's bedroom, the brushing of those wings against the door.

At five-thirty he suggested breakfast, bacon and fried bread, if only to stop the growing look of panic in his wife's eyes and to calm the fretful children. She did not know about the birds upstairs. The bedroom, luckily, was not over the kitchen. Had it been so she could not have failed to hear the sound of them, up there, tapping the boards. And the silly, senseless thud of the suicide birds, the death-and-glory boys, who flew into the bedroom, smashing their heads against the walls. He knew them of old, the herring gulls. They had no brains. The black-backs were different, they knew what they were doing. So did the buzzards, the hawks....

He found himself watching the clock, gazing at the hands that went so slowly round the dial. If his theory was not correct, if the attack did not cease with the turn of the tide, he knew they were beaten. They could not continue through the long day without air, without rest, without more fuel, without ... his mind raced. He knew there were so many things they needed to withstand siege. They were not fully prepared. They were not ready. It might be that it would be safer in the towns after all. If he could get a message through on the farm telephone, to his cousin, only a short journey by train up country, they might be able to hire a car. That would be quicker – hire a car between tides....

His wife's voice, calling his name, drove away the sudden, desperate desire for sleep.

'What is it? What now?' he said sharply.

'The wireless,' said his wife. 'I've been watching the clock. It's nearly seven.'

'Don't twist the knob,' he said, impatient for the first time, 'it's on the Home where it is. They'll speak from the Home.'

They waited. The kitchen clock struck seven. There was no sound. No chimes, no music. They waited until a quarter past, switching to the Light. The result was the same. No news bulletin came through.

'We've heard wrong,' he said, 'they won't be broadcasting until eight o'clock.'

They left it switched on, and Nat thought of the battery,

wondered how much power was left in it. It was generally recharged when his wife went shopping in the town. If the battery failed they would not hear the instructions.

'It's getting light,' whispered his wife, 'I can't see it, but I can feel it. And the birds aren't hammering so loud.'

She was right. The rasping, tearing sound grew fainter every moment. So did the shuffling, the jostling for place upon the step, upon the sills. The tide was on the turn. By eight there was no sound at all. Only the wind. The children, lulled at last by the stillness, fell asleep. At half past eight Nat switched the wireless off.

'What are you doing? We'll miss the news,' said his wife.

'There isn't going to be any news,' said Nat. 'We've got to depend upon ourselves.'

He went to the door and slowly pulled away the barricades. He drew the bolts, and kicking the bodies from the step outside the door breathed the cold air. He had six working hours before him, and he knew he must reserve his strength for the right things, not waste it in any way. Food, and light, and fuel; these were the necessary things. If he could get them in sufficiency, they could endure another night.

He stepped into the garden, and as he did so he saw the living birds. The gulls had gone to ride the sea, as they had done before; they sought sea food, and the buoyancy of the tide, before they returned to the attack. Not so the land birds. They waited and watched. Nat saw them, on the hedgerows, on the soil, crowded in the trees, outside in the field, line upon line of birds, all still, doing nothing.

He went to the end of his small garden. The birds did not move. They went on watching him.

'I've got to get food,' said Nat to himself, 'I've got to go to the farm to find food.'

He went back to the cottage. He saw to the windows and the doors. He went upstairs and opened the children's bedroom. It was empty, except for the dead birds on the floor. The living were out there, in the garden, in the fields. He went downstairs.

'I'm going to the farm,' he said.

His wife clung to him. She had seen the living birds from the open door.

'Take us with you,' she begged, 'we can't stay here alone. I'd rather die than stay here alone.'

He considered the matter. He nodded.

'Come on, then,' he said, 'bring baskets, and Johnny's pram. We can load up the pram.'

The dressed against the biting wind, wore gloves and scarves. His wife put Johnny in the pram. Nat took Jill's hand.

'The birds,' she whimpered, 'they're all out there, in the fields.'

'They won't hurt us,' he said, 'not in the light.'

They started walking across the field towards the stile, and the birds did not move. They waited, their heads turned to the wind.

When they reached the turning to the farm, Nat stopped and told his wife to wait in the shelter of the hedge with the two children.

'But I want to see Mrs Trigg,' she protested. 'There are lots of things we can borrow, if they went to market yesterday; not only bread, and ...'

'Wait here,' Nat interrupted. 'I'll be back in a moment.'

The cows were lowing, moving restlessly in the yard, and he could see a gap in the fence where the sheep had knocked their way through, to roam unchecked in the front garden before the farm-house. No smoke came from the chimneys. He was filled with misgiving. He did not want his wife or the children to go down to the farm.

'Don't jib now,' said Nat, harshly, 'do what I say.'

She withdrew with the pram into the hedge, screening herself and the children from the wind.

He went down alone to the farm. He pushed his way through the herd of bellowing cows, which turned this way and that, distressed, their udders full. He saw the car standing by the gate, not put away in the garage. The windows of the farm-house were smashed. There were many dead gulls lying in the yard and around the house. The living birds perched on the group of trees behind the farm and on the roof of the house. They were quite still. They watched him.

Jim's body lay in the yard ... what was left of it. When the birds had finished, the cows had trampled him. His gun was beside him. The door of the house was shut and bolted, but as the windows were smashed it was easy to lift them and climb through. Trigg's body was close to the telephone. He must have been trying to get through to the exchange when the birds came for him. The receiver was hanging loose, the instrument torn from the wall. No sign of Mrs Trigg. She would be upstairs. Was it any use going up? Sickened, Nat knew what he would find.

'Thank God,' he said to himself, 'there were no children.'

He forced himself to climb the stairs, but half-way he turned and descended again. He could see her legs, protruding from the open bedroom door. Beside her were the bodies of the black-backed gulls, and an umbrella, broken.

'It's no use,' though Nat, 'doing anything. I've only got five hours, less than that. The Triggs would understand. I must load up with what I can find.'

He tramped back to his wife and children.

'I'm going to fill up the car with stuff,' he said. 'I'll put coal in it, and paraffin for the primus. We'll take it home and return for a fresh load.'

'What about the Triggs?' asked his wife.

'They must have gone to friends,' he said.

'Shall I come and help you, then?'

'No; there's a mess down there. Cows and sheep all over the place. Wait, I'll get the car. You can sit in it.'

Clumsily he backed the car out of the yard and into the lane. His wife and the children could not see Jim's body from there.

'Stay here,' he said, 'never mind the pram. The pram can be fetched later. I'm going to load the car.'

Her eyes watched his all the time. He believed she understood, otherwise she would have suggested helping him to find the bread and groceries.

They made three journeys altogether, backwards and forwards between their cottage and the farm, before he was satisfied they had everything they needed. It was surprising, once he started thinking, how many things were necessary. Almost the most important of all was planking for the windows. He had to go round searching for timber. He wanted to renew the boards on all the windows at the cottage. Candles, paraffin, nails, tinned stuff; the list was endless. Besides all that, he milked three of the cows. The rest, poor brutes, would have to go on bellowing.

On the final journey he drove the car to the bus-stop, got out, and went to the telephone box. He waited a few minutes, jangling the receiver. No good, though. The line was dead. He climbed onto a bank and looked over the countryside, but there was no sign of life at all, nothing in the fields but the waiting, watching birds. Some of them slept – he could see the beaks tucked into the feathers.

'You'd think they'd be feeding,' he said to himself, 'not just standing in that way.'

Then he remembered. They were gorged with food. They had eaten their fill during the night. That was why they did not move this morning....

No smoke came from the chimneys of the council houses. He thought of the children who had run across the fields the night before.

'I should have known,' he thought, 'I ought to have taken them home with me.'

He lifted his face to the sky. It was colourless and grey. The bare trees on the landscape looked bent and blackened by the east wind. The cold did not affect the living birds, waiting out there in the fields.

'This is the time they ought to get them,' said Nat, 'they're a sitting target now. They must be doing this all over the country. Why don't our aircraft take off now and spray them with mustard gas? What are all our chaps doing? They must know, they must see for themselves.'

He went back to the car and got into the driver's seat.

'Go quickly past that second gate,' whispered his wife. 'The postman's lying there. I don't want Jill to see.'

He accelerated. The little Morris bumped and rattled along the lane. The children shrieked with laughter.

'Up-a-down, up-a-down,' shouted young Johnny.

It was a quarter to one by the time they reached the cottage. Only an hour to go.

'Better have cold dinner,' said Nat. 'Hot up something for yourself and the children, some of that soup. I've no time to eat now. I've got to unload all this stuff.'

He got everything inside the cottage. It could be sorted later. Give them all something to do during the long hours ahead. First he must see to the windows and the doors.

He went round the cottage methodically, testing every window, every door. He climbed onto the roof also, and fixed boards across every chimney, except the kitchen. The cold was so intense he could hardly bear it, but the job had to be done. Now and again he would look up, searching the sky for aircraft. None came. As he worked he cursed the inefficiency of the authorities.

'It's always the same,' he muttered, 'they always let us down. Muddle, muddle, from the start. No plan, no real organization. And we don't matter, down here. That's what it is. The people up country have priority. They're using gas up there, no doubt, and all the aircraft. We've got to wait and take what comes.'

He paused, his work on the bedroom chimney finished, and looked out to sea. Something was moving out there. Something grey and white amongst the breakers.

'Good old Navy,' he said, 'they never let us down. They're coming down channel, they're turning in the bay.'

He waited, straining his eyes, watering in the wind, towards the sea. He was wrong, though. It was not ships. The Navy was not there. The gulls were rising from the sea. The massed flocks in the fields, with ruffled feathers, rose in formation from the ground, and wing to wing soared upwards to the sky.

The tide had turned again.

Nat climbed down the ladder and went inside the kitchen. The family were at dinner. It was a little after two. He bolted the door, put up the barricade, and lit the lamp.

'It's night-time,' said young Johnny.

His wife had switched on the wireless once again, but no sound came from it.

'I've been all round the dial,' she said, 'foreign stations, and that lot. I can't get anything.'

'Maybe they have the same trouble,' he said, 'maybe it's the same right through Europe.'

She poured out a plateful of the Triggs' soup, cut him a large slice of the Triggs' bread, and spread their dripping upon it.

They ate in silence. A piece of the dripping ran down young Johnny's chin and fell onto the table.

'Manners, Johnny,' said Jill, 'you should learn to wipe your mouth.'

The tapping began at the windows, at the door. The rustling, the jostling, the pushing for position on the sills. The first thud of the suicide gulls upon the step.

'Won't America do something?' said his wife. 'They've always been our allies, haven't they? Surely America will do something?'

Nat did not answer. The boards were strong against the windows, and on the chimneys too. The cottage was filled with stores, with fuel, with all they needed for the next few days. When he had finished dinner he would put the stuff away, stack it neatly, get everything shipshape, handy-like. His wife could help him, and the children too. They'd tire themselves out, between now and a quarter to nine, when the tide would ebb; then he'd tuck them down on their mattresses, see that they slept good and sound until three in the morning.

He had a new scheme for the windows, which was to fix barbed wire in front of the boards. He had brought a great roll of it from the farm. The nuisance was, he'd have to work at this in the dark, when the lull came between nine and three. Pity he had not thought of it before. Still, as long as the wife slept, and the kids, that was the main thing.

The smaller birds were at the window now. He recognised the light tap-tapping of their beaks, and the soft brush of their wings. The hawks ignored the windows. They concentrated their attack upon the door. Nat listened to the tearing sound of splintering wood, and wondered how many million years of memory were stored in those little brains, behind the stabbing beaks, the piercing eyes, now giving them this instinct to destroy mankind with all the deft precision of machines.

'I'll smoke that last fag,' he said to his wife. 'Stupid of me, it was the one thing I forgot to bring back from the farm.'

He reached for it, switched on the silent wireless. He threw the empty packet on the fire, and watched it burn.

Poor Ash

Richard Adams

To anyone coming up over the lower paddock to the beginning of the lawn, Poor Ash presented, in certain lights, an oddly disturbing appearance, as if watching – with a kind of idiot gaze – the sun set across the three counties. He hesitated as he emerged from the trees and looked up at the house. A heavy calm had settled over the place. Hardly a breeze, the trees making only the vaguest gestures to the deepening blue of the evening. He could hear clearly the voices of the others below – the crash and scramble of the dog in the thicket. 'Here, boy! Here!' Female laughter etched on the silence.

Poor Ash. Solitary, spellbound house. Even its name seemed to crave sympathy. Its topmost windows, bloodshot with their reflections of the sunset sky, seemed to brood over the valley with a mindless stare; the central porch, its thickening shadows seeping onto the upper edge of the lawn, mouthed a cry of anguish to an unhearing world. It was as if a giant – in some savage act of ritual punishment – had been buried upright in the hill, his head alone remaining above the surface, his face fixed in an expression of impotent protest.

In a sudden flurry of dew from the long grass, the dog raced – stick in mouth – out of the copse to his right. Head low, ears back, tail flying. It described a wild, breathless, grinning arc across the lawn in front of him, then plunged back down the slope towards the unseen callers.

He flicked away his cigarette end.

'Good boy!'

The likeness was suddenly very striking. It was the ivy that did it. The two short cottage-wings of the house – simple, one-floor additions, a room apiece, that supported like heraldic beasts Poor Ash's main, rather top-heavy, central structure – were almost completely shrouded in it. It had climbed from both sides inwards and upwards, over the cottages, onto the gable-ends and roof of the house, where it had steadily established itself, feeling its way between the tiles into the blanching gloom of the loft-space. The shock of stalks and leaves that crowned the building, the tumble of creeper hanging listlessly over the eaves – fringing the upper windows, draping the walls – was a luxuriant head of hair from which the colour was now being drained by the advancing twilight.

And there was the honeysuckle. It had been trained up and around the open mouth of the porch, so that it now reached to and curled over the sill of the bay window to the room – his room – that projected over the porch. He had raised the lower sash before coming out with the others. Despite the lack of breeze, the heady sweet perfume of the honeysuckle would be drifting into the room in which he would soon be sleeping.

He turned to the valley and yawned comfortably.

Shadows were drawing round the sky. Pools of pale mist hung in the mid-distance. It was a perfect evening.

Voices again, nearer now. He felt vaguely impatient at the prospect of their catching him up. For the time being, he preferred the company of his own thoughts. He looked back to the house and started his slow progress up the slope of the lawn.

No. Not honeysuckle. More like a moustache – a morose Celtic moustache. Oiled and sweet-smelling. Bizarre.

The dog was with him again, dancing round his feet and coughing importunately. He walked a little more purposefully, in part to discourage the animals's attentions and in part to maintain a lead over the others. As he came up to the gravel path outside the glass-fronted door, he noticed something odd. It couldn't have been the reflection of the sunset he had seen in the top windows from the edge of the

49

paddock. The light, even though he had shifted his angle of vision, was still there. He felt sure that it was coming from inside the rooms. Both rooms. He stood for a moment and gazed up at the dull, reddish patches of light. The floor above his. Someone must have left the lights on.

But both rooms?

The rest of the face was in darkness, his own window over the porch solitarily sniffing at the drowsing honeysuckle, those on the ground floor closely shuttered since the afternoon heat.

He followed the clicking trot of the dog over the tiled threshold into the house.

He shifted.

The pillows troubled him. Barely raising his head, he hooked back his arms and aimed expert simultaneous thumps into their unresisting flanks.

No good.

He tried not to think how long he had not been asleep. He had left the others comparing schools and holidays about half an hour after returning to the house. For a while after coming up he had been aware of the dull buzz of their conversation below. Then nothing. Then feet overhead. And doors. Before drifting off again.

No good at all.

He opened his eyes. They were as he had left them – the moon-filled room, his clothes draped exhausted over the back of a chair, the fine gauze of the curtains blowing serenely. Downstairs, muffled, the dog murmured dreamily. Something else.

He turned his head slightly on the pillow. They were his own noises – the trickling gurgle of his stomach, his cheek grazing the folded-over sheet. He closed his eyes in an effort of concentration. The honeysuckle rustled. To his disembodied right, his watch ticked primly.

Still something else.

He raised himself suddenly onto one elbow and peered

beyond the end of the bed, towards the open window. That was it. The breeze must have sprung up in the last few minutes. That was what was worrying him – after the utter stillness of the evening, he had been roused by the to-and-fro rhythmic sway of the curtains and of the straggling profusion of foliage on the windowsill. They moved to a soft sigh – distant but regular, like a deep contented breathing – now floated towards him into the room, now pressed hard against the panes and billowed out over the porch. The sound, though, seemed to be coming not from the region of the curtains, but here, from somewhere near the bed. By way of experiment, he adjusted his own breathing to the rhythm of the sigh – as if the action of his lungs were sustaining the languid dance at the window. Half-fascinated, he breathed for a while in careful, exaggerated time with the curtains.

No. There was still something wrong.

If the draught was coming – as it ought to be – from one direction, from the garden, from outside, why was the movement both backwards and forwards? The air in the room seemed warm and humid. There was a smell, too – not the powerful fragrance of the honeysuckle, but a stale, musty smell like that of rooms long shut up. And still the hissing sigh. As though he were listening to the breathing of the sleeping house.

Stealthily, he drew up his feet and swung them out of bed. For a moment or two he sat still, as if fearing to disturb the sleeper. Then, with the utmost caution, he edged over to the window, conscious of the cotton swish of his pyjamas and of his light, tacky footfall on the polished boards.

Hiss – sigh. Hiss – sigh. The breathing continued untroubled.

He stood a little to the left of the open window, watching the uncanny, systematic surge of the curtains. He could feel now the strong intermittent fanning of the breeze against his legs and right wrist.

Another experiment: he reached up and placed his fingers on the lower lip of the raised sash. The flaking paintwork was rough to his touch. Was there a slight anxious quickening in the breathing? He couldn't be sure. He drew down the window with a throaty rattle and secured the catch.

Listen.

The sighing had died away. The curtains were still. He peered closely through the glass: the honeysuckle too was motionless.

Moonlight streamed across the silent lawn. It was all beginning to make a weird sort of sense and his fascination was slowly converting to fear. Think. If he really were in a room that breathed, that was alive, then his closing the window amounted to an act of deliberate suffocation. Like a pillow held to the face, a plastic bag over the head.

He shook himself. Ridiculous.

The smell, however, was becoming more intense. A thick, cloying odour of decay. There was an almost physical tension in the air about him. Turning his back on the window, he gazed quickly round the room.

Still. No sound. Not even that of his growing panic – yet an unmistakable sensation of pressure bearing in upon him from all sides. Drops of sweat were beginning to collect in his hair.

Wait! There was something after all. Not in the room though. Distant – deep down somehow – a sort of bubbling gurgle. A choking? He crossed the room swiftly and tried the light switch. Nothing. He put his ear to the door. Now there was desperation in the sound – a sustained rasping groan, increasing in pitch and volume by the second. It seemed to be coming from the room beneath – the large half-panelled hall in which the chief life of the household was carried on and from which the stairs led both up, to his and the other two bedrooms, and down, to the cool damp of the cellar. Transfixed, he listened as new sounds were added to the rising hysteria of the groans. It was if some superhuman force were trying to shake the front door open from the inside. The floor began to vibrate beneath his feet – imperceptibly at first, but within moments as if a gigantic engine had gone berserk and was about to tear the building down about his ears. The whole house shuddered under the enormous stress. The noise was deafening — he covered his ears to reduce the pain. The pressure and heat were unbearable. From the stairs outside his room came the sharp reports of splitting timber. The door handle rattled convulsively. Poor Ash was destroying itself, tearing itself apart in a fit of monstrous torment.

He hurled himself over to the window and threw it open.

The silence was immediate and shattering, as if the house's outburst of anguish and rage had been cut off in mid-sentence. The long moonlight sloped across the lawn. Below, in the paddock, grey shadows of trees stood motionless. He slid to his knees, resting his quivering weight on the window-ledge, gulping at the warm, friendly air. So intense was his relief that for minutes he didn't even try to reason, to explain to himself what had been happening. He waited now for a return of his own calm, gazing at the still, unchanging garden. He felt comforted.

The honeysuckle brushed his moist arm reassuringly. The curtain stroked the length of his back with a soothing, tender touch. Hiss — sigh. Hiss — sigh.

He stiffened. It had not finished!

He must get back to the bed, away from the window — must get once more behind the breathing, away from that sinister to-and-fro movement! But something in the garden caught his attention. Unchanging? No. There was something below him on the lawn.

Lights?

Not the pale radiance of the moon, but warmer, mellower. Two of them. Two identical oblongs of light lying on the grass at right angles to the house. In his tense, confused state it took him longer than would have been usual to realize that they emanated from the rooms on the floor above. The others must have been woken by the noise too. He must talk to them — he couldn't think why he hadn't called out to them before! But he didn't move. Somehow the lights held him. A shadow passed over the one to the right — the magnified outline of a man's head and torso. What had they made of it all?

Still the breathing continued to caress his shoulders. His damp hair stirred slightly in time with the curtains.

Suddenly the lights went out — just for a moment, both at once. Not long, barely a second. Then they were there again, looking up at him with that fixed mesmeric gaze. He swallowed slowly. He could feel the mounting palpitation of his fear high in his chest. Once more the lights went out — again simultaneously, but this time twice in rapid succession. Then again the expressionless stare. The outline figure returned, now blocking out most of the oblong — arms outstretched, hands reaching for the almost invisible line where top and bottom windows met. It was as if the blank, impersonal silhouette were trying to attract attention — either that or else struggling to open the window, and struggling indeed with feverish vigour. Another sequence of blinks and the shadow was gone, like a speck of dust cleared from an eye by the rapid closing and opening of its lid.

Now he knew the reason for his returning terror — as certainly as the window of this room was Poor Ash's nose, those of the two on the floor above were its eyes. He thought of how the house had appeared earlier in the evening: the face of a giant buried upright in the hill. A giant that was very much alive!

He pushed himself to his feet and crossed hastily to the door. He must go and see what was happening upstairs. Perhaps the company of the others would help to nerve him against the fear that was building relentlessly within him.

Only the door wouldn't open!

There was no keyhole and he could make the handle turn all right, but the door wouldn't budge. He tugged savagely, twisting the handle with all his force. He looked about for something with which to gouge between the door and its frame. There was a heavy, electroplate paper-knife on the table to one side of the bed. He set about driving it, with surprising nervous energy, into the slit beside the lock, chipping and scratching the paintwork in the process: he grunted as he worked. He cursed the gloom. Perhaps the light was working again by now? No. He jabbed blindly, still tugging at the handle as he did so. A wordless snarl rose in the back of his throat, and, hurling the paper-knife behind him, he took to pummelling the door with his clenched fists. There flashed into his mind the image of the silhouette he had watched from his window, acting out its frantic drama on the lawn.

So that was it!

He stopped battering. They were all trapped — victims of an enraged, a malign house-spirit! He sank despairing onto the edge of the bed. The noise of his activities seemed not to have carried to any other part of the building. All was still again, except for the sickening drawl of the honeysuckle and the curtains, and for the ghastly sigh.

Outside, the night was seamless.

The chilling scream that rose from below had him on his feet again within seconds. It was not, he thought, a human scream — rather the yodelling howl of a terrified animal. It was followed by an enormous crash and the sound of glass shattering. He lurched first to the window, then back to the door in a renewed burst of hopeless frenzy.

What was he to do?

He hovered, tense, trembling, his eyes wide with fear.

What to do?

Without thinking, he took hold of the door handle. Some force that seemed to be no part of himself made it turn under his hand. And the door opened. It swung weightlessly towards him. In a supreme effort of control, he held it just an inch or so ajar. Listen.

Silence?

He must master this trembling of his arms, his shoulders. Must master the tightness in the pit of his stomach. He wiped his hands down the loose front of his pyjama jacket. Must keep perfectly still. Now. Take a deep breath.

By slow degrees he retrieved a piece of his composure. Listen again.

Silence.

But how? Surely not. He turned again to the open window. The curtains were still. There was no longer any trace of the breathing. Even the drifting motion of the honeysuckle had ceased. Cautiously, he advanced halfway across the room to take a closer look. No movement. No sound. He returned to the door.

The nightmare – was it really over? He reached for the switch. Light flooded the room, paining his eyes.

He opened the door wider and stepped gingerly onto the landing. It was in darkness, but he soon became aware of voices from above and of other doors opening. Another light came on. The stairs sprang to glowing life – no sign of damage, no gaping holes – he was thankful for the solid certainty of their shelving descent into the darkness.

Only there was a smell, a recognizable if faint staleness in the air.

The others came down to where he waited. They were all visibly shaken. Someone offered him a cigarette.

His memory of what followed was rather confused, at least as far as the discussion on the landing was concerned. He didn't speak. He couldn't quite bring himself to believe that it was all over. Warily, he leaned back against the wall and watched their whispering mouths, their drawn and frightened faces. He seemed to be the focus of a rising swell of bewildered conjecture. Voices overlapped. Possibilities and fragments of possibilities swirled about him, so that he could not be certain who was saying what. In his numbed state, he even began to be unsure of how much he had experienced for himself and how much was being recounted by those urgent, twisting lips. He started to shiver.

Suddenly they were all silent again. They knew they must go downstairs.

They would go together. To see.

They hesitated into the darkness. One of the girls tripped on something near the bottom and slithered down the last few stairs, clutching at her husband as she went. The noise was somehow reassuring. Someone put on the light.

The room was almost totally wrecked.

Remains of several small tables and chairs lay scattered at large, their limbs twisted and broken. The much-admired oriental rugs, together with a couple of blue silk cushions (one ripped and gaping) had been tumbled into a heap on the near side of the room. They had been splashed and stained with some dark, treacly substance. One of the curtains had been dragged to the floor; the others hung in tatters. A heavy ceramic lamp-base had been smashed in the hearth, its buckled shade having come to rest over by one of the windows. Books were everywhere, pages splayed and torn, backs broken. The record-player had destroyed itself against the bottom stair. The polished surface of the floor had been scored and disfigured with irregular, huge scratches. It too was streaked liberally with the thick, dark liquid. The massive chesterfield had been hurled back against the wall and apparently subjected to a downward pressure so immense that its feet had collapsed; its belly had been slashed in several places.

The smell of decay he had detected upstairs hung hideous and overpowering in the air.

There was glass everywhere.

Someone thought to look for the dog. One by one, they advanced into the desolation.

It seemed, indeed, as if all the glass in the room had been cracked or broken – ashtrays, ornaments, pictures. All that remained in the shuttered windows and in the massive frame of the front door were long vicious slivers, projecting at crazy angles like a vast, inescapable circle of bared and snarling teeth. Some of these too were stained and had caught at odd intervals between them what on closer examination were revealed to be tufts of coarse, black hair.

It was just inside the door that they found part of the dog: it might have been a leg, but they couldn't be sure. Just a matted lump of skin and sinew from which there winked random splinters of gleaming bone. The rest of the animal they found, at the end of its trail of stains, chewed and nauseous, gulped to the foot of the cellar steps.

A School Story

M. R. James

Two men in a smoking-room were talking of their private-school days. 'At *our* school,' said A, 'we had a ghost's footmark on the staircase. What was it like? Oh, very unconvincing. Just the shape of a shoe, with a square toe, if I remember right. The staircase was a stone one. I never heard any story about the thing. That seems odd, when you come to think of it. Why didn't somebody invent one, I wonder?'

'You never can tell with little boys. They have a mythology of their own. There's a subject for you, by the way – "The Folklore of Private Schools".'

'Yes; the crop is rather scanty, though. I imagine, if you were to investigate the cycle of ghost stories, for instance, which the boys at private schools tell each other, they would all turn out to be highly-compressed versions of stories out of books.'

'Nowadays the *Strand* and *Pearson*'s, and so on, would be extensively drawn upon.'

'No doubt: they weren't born or thought of in *my* time. Let's see. I wonder if I can remember the staple ones that I was told. First, there was the house with a room in which a series of people insisted on passing a night; and each of them in the morning was found kneeling in a corner, and had just time to say, "I've seen it," and died.'

'Wasn't that the house in Berkeley Square?'

'I dare say it was. Then there was the man who heard a noise in the passage at night, opened his door, and saw someone crawling towards him on all fours with his eye hanging out on his cheek. There was besides, let me think –

Yes! the room where a man was found dead in bed with a horseshoe mark on his forehead, and the floor under the bed was covered with marks of horseshoes also; I don't know why. Also there was the lady who, on locking her bedroom door in a strange house, heard a thin voice among the bed-curtains say, "Now we're shut in for the night." None of those had any explanation or sequel. I wonder if they go on still, those stories.'

'Oh, likely enough – with additions from the magazines, as I said. You never heard, did you, of a real ghost at a private school? I thought not; nobody has that ever I came across.'

'From the way in which you said that, I gather that *you* have.'

'I really don't know; but this is what was in my mind. It happened at my private school thirty odd years ago, and I haven't any explanation of it.

'The school I mean was near London. It was established in a large and fairly old house – a great white building with very fine grounds about it; there were large cedars in the garden, as there are in so many of the older gardens in the Thames valley, and ancient elms in the three or four fields which we used for our games. I think probably it was quite an attractive place, but boys seldom allow that their schools possess any tolerable features.

'I came to the school in a September, soon after the year 1870; and among the boys who arrived on the same day was one whom I took to: a Highland boy, whom I will call McLeod. I needn't spend time in describing him: the main thing is that I got to know him very well. He was not an exceptional boy in any way – not particularly good at books or games – but he suited me.

'The school was a large one: there must have been from 120 to 130 boys there as a rule, and so a considerable staff of masters was required, and there were rather frequent changes among them.

'One term – perhaps it was my third or fourth – a new master made his appearance. His name was Sampson. He was a tallish, stoutish, pale, black-bearded man. I think we liked him: he had travelled a good deal, and had stories which amused us on our school walks, so that there was some competition among us to get within earshot of him. I remember too – dear me, I have hardly thought of it since then! – that he had a charm on his watch-chain that attracted my attention one day, and he let me examine it. It was, I now suppose, a gold Byzantine coin; there was an effigy of some absurd emperor on one side; the other side had been worn practically smooth, and he had had cut on it – rather barbarously – his own initials, G. W. S., and a date, 24 July, 1865. Yes, I can see it now: he told me he had picked it up in Constantinople: it was about the size of a florin, perhaps rather smaller.

'Well, the first odd thing that happened was this. Sampson was doing Latin grammar with us. One of his favourite methods – perhaps it is rather a good one – was to make us construct sentences out of our own heads to illustrate the rules he was trying to make us learn. Of course that is a thing which gives a silly boy a chance of being impertinent: there are lots of school stories in which that happens – or anyhow there might be. But Sampson was too good a disciplinarian for us to think of trying that on with him. Now, on this occasion he was telling us how to express *remembering* in Latin: and he ordered us each to make a sentence bringing in the verb *memini*, "I remember". Well, most of us made up some ordinary sentence such as "I remember my father," or "He remembers his book," or something equally uninteresting: and I dare say a good many put down *memino librum meum*, and so forth: but the boy I mentioned – McLeod – was evidently thinking of something more elaborate than that. The rest of us wanted to have our sentences passed, and get on to something else, so some kicked him under the desk, and I, who was next to him, poked him and whispered to him to look sharp. But he didn't seem to attend. I looked at his paper and saw he had put down nothing at all. So I jogged him again harder than before and upbraided him sharply for keeping us all waiting. That did have some effect. He started and seemed to wake up, and then very quickly he scribbled about a couple of lines on his paper, and showed it up with the rest. As it was the last, or nearly the last, to come in, and as Sampson had a good deal to say to the boys who had written *meminiscimus patri meo* and the rest of it, it turned out that the clock struck twelve before he had got to McLeod, and McLeod had to wait afterwards to have his sentence corrected. There was nothing much going on outside when I got out, so I waited for him to come. He came very slowly when he did arrive, and I guessed there had been some sort of trouble. "Well," I said, "what did you get?" "Oh, I don't know," said McLeod, "nothing much: but I think Sampson's rather sick with me." "Why, did you show him up some rot?" "No fear," he said. "It was all right as far as I could see: it was like this: *Memento* – that's right enough for remember, and it takes a genitive, – *memento putei inter quatuor taxos*." "What silly rot!" I said. "What made you shove that down? What does it mean?" "That's the funny part," said McLeod. "I'm not quite sure what it does mean. All I know is, it just came into my head and I corked it down. I know what I *think* it means, because just before I wrote it down I had a sort of picture of it in my head: I believe it means 'Remember the well among the four' – what are those dark sort of trees that have red berries on them?" "Mountain ashes, I s'pose you mean." "I never heard of them," said McLeod; "no, *I'll* tell you – yews." "Well, and what did Sampson say?" "Why, he was jolly odd about it. When he read it he got up and went to the mantelpiece and stopped quite a long time without saying anything, with his back to me. And then he said, without turning round, and rather quiet, 'What do you suppose that means?' I told him what I thought; only I couldn't remember the name of the silly tree: and then he wanted to know why I put it down, and I had to say something or other. And after that he left off talking about it, and asked me how long I'd been here, and where my people lived, and things like that: and then I came away: but he wasn't looking a bit well."

'I don't remember any more that was said by either of us about this. Next day McLeod took to his bed with a chill or something of the kind, and it was a week or more before he was in school again. And as much as a month went by without anything happening that was noticeable. Whether or not Mr Sampson was really startled, as McLeod had thought, he didn't show it. I am pretty sure, of course, now, that there was something very curious in his past history, but I'm not going to pretend that we boys were sharp enough to guess any such thing.

'There was one other incident of the same kind as the last which I told you. Several times since that day we had had to make up examples in school to illustrate different rules, but there had never been any row except when we did them wrong. At last there came a day when we were going through those dismal things which people call Conditional Sentences, and we were told to make a conditional sentence, expressing a future consequence. We did it, right or wrong, and showed up our bits of paper, and Sampson began looking through them. All at once he got up, made some odd sort of noise in his throat, and rushed out by a door that was just by his desk. We sat there for a minute or two, and then − I suppose it was incorrect − but we went up, I and one or two others, to look at the papers on his desk. Of course I thought someone must have put down some nonsense or other, and Sampson had gone off to report him. All the same, I noticed that he hadn't taken any of the papers with him when he ran out. Well, the top paper on the desk was written in red ink − which no one used − and it wasn't in anyone's hand who was in the class. They all looked at it − McLeod and all − and took their dying oaths that it wasn't theirs. Then I thought of counting the bits of paper. And of this I made quite certain: that there were seventeen bits of paper on the desk, and sixteen boys in the form. Well, I bagged the extra paper, and kept it, and I believe I have it now. And now you will want to know what was written on it. It was simple enough, and harmless enough, I should have said.

' "*Si tu non veneris ad me, ego veniam ad te,*" which means, I suppose, "If you don't come to me, I'll come to you." '

'Could you show me the paper?' interrupted the listener.

'Yes, I could: but there's another odd thing about it. That same afternoon I took it out of my locker – I know for certain it was the same bit, for I made a fingermark on it – and no single trace of writing of any kind was there on it. I kept it, as I said, and since that time I have tried various experiments to see whether synthetic ink had been used, but absolutely without result.

'So much for that. After about half an hour Sampson looked in again: said he had felt very unwell, and told us we might go. He came rather gingerly to his desk and gave just one look at the uppermost paper: and I suppose he thought he must have been dreaming: anyhow, he asked no questions.

'That day was a half-holiday, and next day Sampson was in school again, much as usual. That night the third and last incident in my story happened.

'We – McLeod and I – slept in a dormitory at right angles to the main building. Sampson slept in the main building on the first floor. There was a very bright full moon. At an hour which I can't tell exactly, but some time between one and two, I was woken up by somebody shaking me. It was McLeod; and a nice state of mind he seemed to be in. "Come," he said, – "come! there's a burglar getting in through Sampson's window." As soon as I could speak, I said, "Well, why not call out and wake everybody up?" "No, no," he said, "I'm not sure who it is: don't make a row: come and look." Naturally I came and looked, and naturally there was no one there. I was cross enough, and should have called McLeod plenty of names: only – I couldn't tell why – it seemed to me that there *was* something wrong – something that made me very glad I wasn't alone to face it. We were still at the window looking out, and as soon as I could, I asked him what he had heard or seen. "I didn't *hear* anything at all," he said, "but about five minutes before I woke you, I found myself looking out of this window here, and there was a man sitting or kneeling on Sampson's window-sill, and looking in, and I thought he was beckoning." "What sort of man?" McLeod wriggled. "I don't know," he said, "but I can tell you one thing — he was beastly thin: and he looked as if he was wet all over: and," he said, looking round and whispering as if he hardly liked to hear himself, "I'm not at all sure that he was alive."

'We went on talking in whispers some time longer and eventually crept back to bed. No one else in the room woke or stirred the whole time. I believe we did sleep a bit afterwards, but we were very cheap next day.

'And next day Mr Sampson was gone: not to be found: and I believe no trace of him has ever come to light since. In thinking it over, one of the oddest things about it all has seemed to me to be the fact that neither McLeod nor I ever mentioned what we had seen to any third person whatever. Of course no questions were asked on the subject, and if they had been, I am inclined to believe that we could not have made any answer: we seemed unable to speak about it.

'That is my story,' said the narrator. 'The only approach to a ghost story connected with a school that I know, but still, I think, an approach to such a thing.'

The sequel to this may perhaps be reckoned highly conventional; but a sequel there is, and so it must be produced. There had been more than one listener to the story, and, in the latter part of that same year, or of the next, one such listener was staying at a country house in Ireland.

One evening his host was turning over a drawer full of odds and ends in the smoking-room. Suddenly he put his hand upon a little box. 'Now,' he said, 'you know about old things; tell me what that is.' My friend opened the little box, and found in it a thin gold chain with an object attached to it. He glanced at the object and then took off his spectacles to examine it more narrowly. 'What's the history of this?' he asked. 'Odd enough,' was the answer. 'You know the yew thicket in the shrubbery: well, a year or two back we were cleaning out the old well that used to be in the clearing here, and what do you suppose we found?'

'Is it possible that you found a body?' said the visitor, with an odd feeling of nervousness.

'We did that: but what's more, in every sense of the word, we found two.'

'Good Heavens! Two? Was there anything to show how they got there? Was this thing found with them?'

'It was. Amongst the rags of the clothes that were on one of the bodies. A bad business, whatever the story of it may have been. One body had the arms tight round the other. They must have been there thirty years or more — long enough before we came to this place. You may judge we filled the well up fast enough. Do you make anything of what's cut on that gold coin you have there?'

'I think I can,' said my friend, holding it to the light (but he read it without much difficulty); 'it seems to be G. W. S., 24 July, 1865.'

The Empty Schoolroom

Pamela Hansford Johnson

My mother and father were in India and I had no aunts, uncles or cousins with whom I could spend my holidays; so I stayed behind in the drab and echoing school to amuse myself as best I could, my only companions the housekeeper, the maid, and Mademoiselle Fournier, who also had nowhere else to go.

Our school was just outside the village of Bellançay, which is in the North of France, four or five kilometres from Rouen. It was a tall, narrow house set upon the top of a hill, bare save for the great sweep of beech trees sheltering the long carriage drive. As I look back some twenty-seven years to my life there, it seems to me that the sun never shone, that the grass was always dun-coloured beneath a dun-coloured sky, and that the vast spaces of the lawns were broken perpetually by the scurry of dry brown leaves licked along by a small bitter wind. This inaccurate impression remains with me because, I suppose, I was never happy at Bellançay. There were twenty or thirty other girls there – French, German or Swiss; I was the only English girl among them. Madame de Vallon, the headmistress, did not love my nation. She could not forget that she had been born in 1815, the year of defeat. With Mademoiselle Maury, the young assistant teacher, I was a little more at ease, for she, even if she did not care for me, had too volatile a nature not to smile and laugh sometimes, even for the benefit of those who were not her favourites.

Mademoiselle Fournier was a dependent cousin of our headmistress. She was in her late fifties, a little woman dry as a winter twig, her face very tight, small and wary under a wig of coarse yellow hair. To pay for her board and lodging she taught deportment: in her youth she had been at the Court of the Tzar, and it was said that at sixteen years of age she was betrothed to a Russian nobleman. There was some sort of mystery here, about which all the girls were curious. Louise de Chausson said her mother had told her the story – how the nobleman, on the eve of his wedding, had shot himself through the head, having received word that certain speculations in which he had for many years been involved had come to light, and that his arrest was imminent.... 'And from that day,' Louise whispered, her prominent eyes gleaming in the candlelight, 'she began to wither and wither and wither away, till all her beauty was gone....' Yes, I can see Louise now, kneeling upon her bed at the end of the vast dormitory, her thick plait hanging down over her nightgown, the little cross with the turquoise glittering at her beautiful and grainy throat. The others believed the story implicitly, except the piece about Mademoiselle Fournier's lost beauty. That they could not stomach. No, she was ugly as a monkey and had always been so.

For myself, I disbelieved in the nobleman; believed in the beauty. I have always had a curious faculty for stripping age from a face, recognising the structure of the bone and the original texture of the skin beneath the disguisings of blotch, red vein and loosened flesh. When I looked at Mademoiselle Fournier I saw that the pinched and veinous nose had once been delicate and fine; that the sunken eyes had once been almond-shaped and blue; that the small, loose mouth had once pouted charmingly and opened upon romantic words. Why did I not believe in the nobleman? For no better reason than a distrust of Louise's information on any conceivable point. She was a terrible teller of falsehoods.

I was seventeen years old when I spent my last vacation at Bellançay, and knowing that my parents were to return to Europe in the following spring I watched the departure of the other girls with a heart not quite so heavy as was usual upon these occasions. In six months' time I, too, would be welcomed and loved, have adventures to relate and hopes upon which to feed.

I waved to them from a dormer window as they rattled away in fiacre and barouche down the drive between the beech trees, sired and damed, uncled and aunted, their boxes stacked high and their voices high as the treetops. They had never before seemed to me a particularly attractive group of girls – that is, not in the mass. There was, of course, Hélène de Courcey, with her great olive eyes; Madeleine Millet, whose pale red hair hung to her knees; but in the cluster they had no particular charm. That day, however, as, in new bonnets flowered and feathered and gauzed, they passed from sight down the narrowing file of beeches, I thought them all beautiful as princesses, and as princesses fortunate. Perhaps the nip in the air of a grey June made their cheeks rose-red, their eyes bright as the eyes of desirable young ladies in ballrooms.

The last carriage disappeared, the last sound died away. I turned from the window and went down the echoing stairs, flight after flight to the *salle-à-manger*, where my luncheon awaited me.

I ate alone. Mademoiselle Fournier took her meals in her own room upon the second floor, reading as she ate, crumbs falling from her lip onto the page. Tonight she and I, in the pattern of all holiday nights, would sit together for a while in the drawing room before retiring.

'You don't make much of a meal, I must say,' Marie, the maid, rebuked me, as she cleared the plates. 'You can't afford to grow thinner, Mademoiselle, or you'll snap in two.' She brought me some cherries, which I would not eat then but preferred to take out with me in the garden. 'I'll wrap them up for you. No! you can't put them in your handkerchief like that; you'll stain it.'

She chattered to me for a while, in her good nature trying to ease my loneliness. Marie, at least, had relations in the village with whom she sometimes spent her evenings. 'What are you going to do with yourself, eh? Read your eyes out as usual?'

'I shall walk this afternoon, unless I find it too chilly.'

'You'll find it raining,' said Marie, cocking a calculating eye towards the high windows, 'in an hour. No, less; in half an hour.'

She busied herself wrapping up my cherries, which she handed to me in a neat parcel with a firm fingerloop of string. 'If it's wet you can play the piano.'

'You've forgotten,' I said, 'we have none now, or shan't have till they send the new one.'

Madame de Vallon had recently sold the old instrument, ugly and tinny, and with the money from the sale plus some money raised by parents' subscription had bought a grand pianoforte from Monsieur Oury, the mayor, whose eldest daughter, the musical one, had lately died.

'You can play on Mademoiselle Fournier's,' said Marie, 'she won't mind. You go and ask her.'

'What, is there another piano in the school?' I was amazed. I had been at Bellançay for seven years and had fancied no corner of the building unknown to me.

'Ah-ha,' said Marie triumphantly, 'there are still things you don't know, eh? You don't have to do the housework, or you'd be wiser.'

'But where is it?'

'In the empty schoolroom.'

I laughed at her. 'But they're all empty now! Whatever do you mean?'

'The one at the top,' she said impatiently, 'the one up the little flight of four stairs.'

'But that's the lumber room!'

'There's lumber in it. But it was a schoolroom once. It was when my aunt worked here. The piano's up there still, though *she* never plays it now.' Marie jerked her head skywards to indicate Mademoiselle Fournier upstairs.

I was fascinated by this information. We girls had never entered the lumber room because no attraction had been attached to it: to us it was simply a small, grimy door in the attic, locked we imagined, as we had never seen anyone go in or out. All we knew was that old books, valises, crates of unwanted china, were sometimes stacked up there out of the way.

There! I have failed to make my point quite clear. I must try again. *There was no mystery whatsoever attaching to this room,* which is the reason why no girl had ever tried the handle. Schoolgirls are curious and roaming creatures; how better can they be kept from a certain path than by the positive assurance that it is a *cul-de-sac*?

Dismissing Marie, I determined to go and seek permission from Mademoiselle Fournier to play upon her pianoforte. Since the departure of the old one, I had missed my music lessons and above all my practising; most of the girls were delighted to be saved a labour which to me, though I was an indifferent performer, had never been anything but a pleasure.

Mademoiselle had finished her meal and was just coming out upon the landing as I ran up the stairs to find her. I made my request.

She looked at me. 'Who told you about the instrument?'

'Marie.'

She was silent. Her brows moved up and down, moving the wig as they did so. It was a familiar trick with her when she was puzzled or annoyed. At last she said, without expression, 'No, you may not go up there,' and pushing me, hurried on downstairs.

At the turn of the staircase, however, she stopped and looked up. Her whole face was working with some unrecognizable emotion and her cheeks were burning red. 'Is there *no* place one can keep to oneself?' she cried at me furiously, and ducking her head, ran on.

When we sat that evening in the drawing room, in our chairs turned to the fireless grate, she made no reference to the little scene of that afternoon. I thought she was, perhaps, sorry for having spoken so sharply: for she asked me a few personal questions of a kindly nature and just before bedtime brought out a tin box full of sugared almonds, which she shared with me.

She rose a little before I did, leaving me to retire when I

chose. I stayed for perhaps half an hour in that vast, pale room with its moth-coloured draperies and its two tarnished chandeliers hanging a great way below the ceiling. Then I took up my candle and went to bed.

Now I must insist that I was a docile girl, a little sullen, perhaps, out of an unrealized resentment against my parents for (as I thought) deserting me; but obedient. I never had a bad conduct report from any of our teachers. It is important that this fact should be realized, so the reader shall know that what I did was not of my own free will.

I could not sleep. I lay open-eyed until my candle burned halfway down and the moon shifted round into the windowpane, weaving the golden light with its own blue-silver. I had no thought of any importance. Small pictures from the day's humdrum events flashed across my brain. I saw the neatly-looped parcel of cherries, the currant stain at the hem of Marie's apron, the starch-blue bird on the bonnet of Louise de Chausson, who had left Bellançay to marry an elderly and not very rich nobleman of Provence. I saw the leaves scurrying over the grey lawns, saw a woodpecker rapping at the trunk of the tree behind the house. What I did not see was the face of Mademoiselle Fournier upturned from the stairway. She never entered my thoughts at all.

And so it is very strange that just before dawn I rose up, put on my dressing gown and sought about the room until I found a pair of gloves my father had had made for me in India, fawn-coloured, curiously stitched in gold and dark green thread. These I took up, left the room and made my way silently up through the quiet house till I came to the door of the lumber room – or, as Marie had called it, the empty schoolroom. I paused with my hand upon the latch and listened. There was no sound except the impalpable breathing of the night, compound perhaps of the breathings of all who sleep, or perhaps of the movement of the moon through the gathered clouds.

I raised the latch gently and stepped within the room, closing the door softly behind me.

The chamber ran halfway across the length of the house at the rear of it, and was lighted by a ceiling window through which the moonrays poured lavishly down. It was still a schoolroom, despite the lumber stacked at the far end, the upright piano standing just behind the door. Facing me was a dais, on which stood a table and a chair. Before the dais were row upon row of desks, with benches behind. Everything was very dusty. With my finger I wrote DUST upon the teacher's table, then scuffed the word out again.

I went to the pianoforte. Behind the lattice-work was a ruching of torn red silk; the candle stumps in the sconces were red also. On the rack stood a piece of music, a Chopin nocturne simplified for beginners.

Gingerly I raised the lid and a mottled spider ran across the keys, dropped on hasty thread to the floor and ran away. The underside of the lid was completely netted by his silk; broken strands waved in the disturbed air and over the discoloured keys. As a rule I am afraid of spiders. That night I was not afraid. I laid my gloves on the keyboard, then closed the piano lid upon them.

I was ready to go downstairs. I took one glance about the room and for a moment thought I saw a shadowy form sitting upon one of the back benches, a form that seemed to weep. Then the impression passed away, and there was only the moonlight painting the room with its majesty. I went out, latched the door and crept back to my bed where, in the first colouring of dawn, I fell asleep.

Next day it was fine. I walked to the river in the morning, and in the afternoon worked at my *petit-point* upon the terrace. At teatime an invitation came for me. The mayor, M. Oury, wrote to Mademoiselle Fournier saying he believed there was a young lady left behind at school for the holidays, and that if she would care to dine at his house upon the following evening it would be a great pleasure to him and to his two young daughters. 'We are not a gay house these days,' he wrote, 'but if the young lady cares for books and flowers there are a great number of both in my library and conservatory.'

73

'Shall I go?' I asked her.

'But of course! It is really a great honour for you. Do you know who the mayor's mother was before her marriage? She was a Uzès. Yes. And when she married M. Oury's father, a very handsome man, her family cut her off with nothing at all and never spoke to her again. But they were very happy. You must wear your best gown and your white hat. Take the gown to Marie and she will iron it for you.'

The day upon which I was to visit M. Oury was sunless and chilly. Plainly the blue dress that Marie had so beautifully spotted and pressed would not do at all. I had, however, a gown of fawn-coloured merino, plain but stylish, with which my brown straw hat would look very well.

Mademoiselle Fournier left the house at four o'clock to take tea with the village priest. She looked me over before she went, pinched my dress, tweaked it, pulled out the folds, and told me to sit quite still until the mayor's carriage came for me at half past six. 'Sit like a mouse, mind, or you will spoil the effect. Remember, M. Oury is not nobody.' She said suddenly, 'Where are your gloves?'

I had forgotten them.

'Forgetting the very things that make a lady look a lady! Go and fetch them at once. Marie!'

The maid came in.

'Marie, see Mademoiselle's gloves are nice, and brush her down once more just as you see the carriage enter the drive. I mustn't wait now. Well, Maud, I wish you a pleasant evening. Don't forget you must be a credit to us.'

When she had gone Marie asked for my gloves. 'You'd better wear your brown ones with that hat, Mademoiselle.'

'Oh!' I exclaimed, 'I can't! I lost one of them on the expedition last week.'

'Your black, then?'

'They won't do. They'd look dreadful with this gown and hat. I know! I have a beautiful Indian pair that will match my dress exactly! I'll go and look for them.'

I searched. The reader must believe that I hunted all over

my room for them anxiously, one eye upon the clock, though it was not yet twenty minutes past four. Chagrined, really upset at the thought of having my toilette ruined, I sat down upon the edge of the bed and began to cry a little. Tears came very easily to me in those lost and desolate days.

From high up in the house I heard a few notes of the piano, the melody of a Chopin nocturne played fumblingly in the treble, and I thought at once, 'Of course! The gloves are up there, where I hid them.'

The body warns us of evil before the senses are half awakened. I knew no fear as I ran lightly up towards the empty schoolroom, yet as I reached the door I felt a wave of heat engulf me, and knew a sick, nauseous stirring within my body. The notes, audible only to my ear (not to Marie's, for even at that moment I could hear her calling out some enquiry or gossip to the housekeeper), ceased. I lifted the latch and looked in.

The room appeared to be deserted, yet I could see the presence within it and know its distress. I peeped behind the door.

At the piano sat a terribly ugly, thin young girl in a dunce's cap. She was half turned towards me, and I saw her pig-like profile, the protruding teeth, the spurt of sandy eyelash. She wore a holland dress in the fashion of twenty years ago, and lean yellow streamers of hair fell down over her back from beneath the paper cone. Her hands, still resting on the fouled keyboard, were meshed about with the spider's web; beneath them lay my Indian gloves.

I made a movement towards the girl. She swivelled sharply and looked me full in the face. Her eyes were all white, red-rimmed, but tearless.

To get my gloves I must risk touching her. We looked at each other, she and I, and her head shrank low between her hunching shoulders. Somehow I must speak to her friendlily, disarm her while I gained my objective.

'Was it you playing?' I asked.

No answer. I closed my eyes. Stretching out my hands as

75

in a game of blind man's buff, I sought for the keyboard.

'I have never heard you before,' I said.

I touched something: I did not know whether it was a glove or her dead hand.

'Have you been learning long?' I said. I opened my eyes. She was gone. I took my gloves, dusted off the webs and ran, ran so fast down the well of the house that on the last flight I stumbled and fell breathless into Marie's arms.

'Oh, I have had a fright! I have had a fright!'

She led me into the drawing room, made me lie down, brought me a glass of wine.

'What is it, Mademoiselle? Shall I fetch the housekeeper? What has happened?'

But the first sip of wine had made me wary. 'I thought I saw someone hiding in my bedroom, a man. Perhaps a thief.'

At this the house was roused. Marie, the housekeeper and the gardener, who had not yet finished his work, searched every room (the lumber room, too, I think) but found nothing. I was scolded, petted, dosed, and Marie insisted, when the housekeeper was out of the way, on putting a soupçon of rouge on my cheeks because, she said, I could not upset M. le Maire by looking like a dead body – he, poor man, having so recently had death in his house!

I recovered myself sufficiently to climb into the carriage, when it came, to comport myself decently on the drive, and to greet the mayor and his two daughters with dignity. Dinner, however, was a nightmare. My mind was so full of the horror I had seen that I could not eat – indeed I could barely force my trembling hand to carry the fork to my lips.

The mayor's daughters were only children, eleven and thirteen years old. At eight o'clock he bade them say goodnight to me and prepare for bed. When they had left us I told him I thought I had stayed long enough: but with a very grave look he placed his hand upon my arm and pressed me gently back into my chair.

'My dear young lady,' he said, 'I know your history, I know you are lonely and unhappy in France without your parents. Also I know that you have suffered some violent shock. Will you tell me about it and let me help you?'

The relief of his words, of his wise and kindly gaze, was too much for me. For the first time in seven years I felt fathered and in haven. I broke down and cried tempestuously, and he did not touch me or speak to me till I was a little more calm. Then he rang for the servant and told her to bring some lime-flower tea. When I had drunk and eaten some of the sweet cake that he urged upon me I told him about the empty schoolroom and of the horror which sat there at the webbed piano.

When I had done he was silent for a little while. Then he took both my hands in his.

'Mademoiselle,' he said, 'I am not going to blame you for the sin of curiosity; I think there was some strange compulsion upon you to act as you did. Therefore I mean to shed a little light upon this sad schoolroom by telling you the story of Mademoiselle Fournier.'

I started.

'No,' he continued restrainingly, 'you must listen quietly; and what I tell you you must never repeat to a soul save your own mother until both Mademoiselle Fournier and Madame de Vallon, her cousin, have passed away.'

I have kept this promise. They have been dead some fourteen years.

M. Oury settled back in his chair. A tiny but comforting fire was lit in the grate, and the light of it was like a ring of guardian angels about us.

'Mademoiselle Fournier,' he began, 'was a very beautiful and proud young woman. Although she had no dowry, she was yet considered something of a *partie*, and in her nineteenth year she became affianced to a young Russian nobleman who at that time was living with his family upon an estate near Arles. His mother was not too pleased with the match, but she was a good woman, and she treated Charlotte – that is, Mademoiselle Fournier – with kindness. Just before the marriage Charlotte's father, who had been created a marquis by Bonaparte and now, by tolerance, held a minor government post under Louis Philippe, was found to have embezzled many thousands of francs.'

'Her father!' I could not help but exclaim.

M. Oury smiled wryly. 'Legend has the lover for villain, eh? No; it was Aristide Fournier, a weak man, unable to stomach any recession in his fortunes. M. Fournier shot himself as the gendarmes were on their way to take him. Charlotte, her marriage prospects destroyed, came near to lunacy. When she recovered from her long illness her beauty had gone. The mother of her ex-fiancé, in pity, suggested that a friend of hers, a lady at the Court of the Tzar, should employ Charlotte as governess to her children, and in Russia Charlotte spent nine years. She returned to France to assist her cousin with the school at Bellançay that Madame de Vallon had recently established.'

'Why did she return?' I said, less because I wished to know the answer than because I wished to break out of the veil of the past he was drawing about us both, and to feel myself a reality once more, Maud Arlett, aged seventeen years and nine months, brown hair and grey eyes, five foot seven and a half inches tall.

I did not succeed. The veil tightened, grew more opaque. 'Nobody knows. There were rumours. It seems not improbable that she was dismissed by her employer ... why, I don't know. It is an obscure period in Charlotte's history.'

He paused, to pour more tea for me.

'It was thought at first that Charlotte would be of great assistance to Madame de Vallon, teach all subjects and act as Madame's secretary. It transpired, however, that Charlotte was nervous to the point of sickness, and that she would grow less and less capable of teaching young girls. Soon she had no duties in the school except to give lessons in music and deportment.

'The music room was in the attic, which was then used as a schoolroom also. The pianoforte was Charlotte's own, one of the few things saved from the wreck of her home.'

M. Oury rose and walked out of the ring of firelight. He stood gazing out of the window, now beaded by a thin rain, and his voice grew out of the dusk as the music of waves grows out of the sea. 'I shall tell you the rest briefly, Mademoiselle. It distresses me to tell it to you at all, but I think I can help you in no other way.

'A young girl came to the school, a child; perhaps twelve or thirteen years of age. Her mother and father were in the East, and she was left alone, even during the vacations —'

'Like myself!' I cried.

'Yes, like yourself; and I have an idea that that is why she chose you for her ... *confidante.*'

I shuddered.

He seemed to guess at my movement for, turning from the window, he returned to the firelight and to me.

'In one way, however, she was unlike you as can possibly be imagined, Mademoiselle.' He smiled with a faint, sad gallantry. 'She was exceedingly ugly.

'From the first, Charlotte took a dislike to her, and it grew to mania. The child, Thérèse Dasquier, was never very intelligent; in Charlotte's grip she became almost imbecile. Charlotte was always devising new punishments, new humiliations. Thérèse became the mock and the pity of the school.'

'But Madame de Vallon, couldn't she have stopped it?' I interrupted indignantly.

'My dear,' M. Oury replied sadly, 'like many women of intellect – she is, as you know, a fine teacher – she is blind to most human distress. She is, herself, a kind woman: she believes others are equally kind, cannot believe there could be ... suffering ... torment ... going on beneath her very nose. Has she ever realized *your* loneliness, Mademoiselle, given you any motherly word, or ...? I thought not. But I am digressing, and that I must not do. We have talked too much already.

'One night Thérèse Dasquier arose quietly, crept from the dormitory and walked barefooted a mile and a half in the rain across the fields to the river, where she drowned herself.'

'Oh, God,' I murmured, my heart cold and heavy as a stone.

'God, I think,' said Monsieur Oury, 'cannot have been attentive at that time ...' His face changed. He added hastily, 'And God forgive me for judging Him. We cannot know – we cannot guess ...' he continued rapidly, in a dry, rather high voice oddly unlike his own. 'There was scandal, great scandal. Thérèse's parents returned to France and everyone expected them to force the truth to light. They turned out to be frivolous and selfish people, who could scarcely make even a parade of grief for a child they had never desired and whose death they could not regret. Thérèse was buried and forgotten. Slowly, very slowly, the story also was forgotten. After all, nobody *knew* the truth, they could only make conjecture.'

'Then how did you know?' I cried out.

'Because Madame de Vallon came to me in bitter distress with the tale of the rumours and besought me to clear Charlotte's name. You see, she simply could not believe a word against her. And at the same time the aunt of Marie, the maid, came to me swearing she could prove the truth of the accusations.... Three days afterwards she was killed in the fire which destroyed the old quarter of Bellançay.'

I looked my enquiry into his face.

'I knew which of the women spoke the truth,' he replied, answering me, 'because in Madame de Vallon's face I saw concern for her own blood. In the other woman's I saw concern for a child who to her was nothing.'

'But still, you *guessed*!' I protested.

He turned upon me his long and grave regard. 'You,' he said, '*you* do not know the truth? Even you?'

I do not know how I endured the following weeks in that lonely school. I remember how long I lay shivering in my bed, staring into the flame of the candle because I felt that in the brightest part of it alone was refuge, how the sweat jumped out from my brow at the least sound in the stillness of midnight, and how, towards morning, I would fall into some morose and terrible dream of dark stairways and locked doors.

Yet, as day by day, night by night, went by with no untoward happening, my spirit knew some degree of easing and I began once more to find comfort in prayer – that is, I dared once again to cover my face while I repeated 'Our Father,' and to rise from my knees without fear of what might be standing patiently at my shoulder.

The holidays drew to an end. 'Tomorrow,' said Mademoiselle Fournier, folding her needlework in preparation for bed, 'your companions will be back with you once more. You'll like that, eh?'

Ever since my request and her refusal, she had been perfectly normal in her manner – I mean, she had been normally sour, polite, withdrawn.

'I shall like it,' I sighed, 'only too well.'

She smiled remotely. 'I am not a lively companion for you, Maud, I fear. Still, I am as I am. I am too old to change myself.'

She went on upstairs, myself following, our candles smoking in the draught and our shadows prancing upon the wall.

I said my prayers and read for a little while. I was unusually calm, feeling safety so nearly within my reach that I need be in no hurry to stretch out my hand and grasp it tight. The bed seemed softer than usual, the sheets sweet-smelling, delicately warm and light. I fell into a dreamless sleep.

I awoke suddenly to find the moon full on my face. I sat up, dazzled by her light, a strange feeling of energy tingling in my body. 'What is it,' I whispered, 'that I must do?'

The moon shone broadly on the great surfaces of gleaming wood, on the bureau, the tallboy, the wardrobe, flashed upon the mirror, sparkled on the spiralling bedposts. I slipped out of bed and in my nightgown went out into the passage.

It was very bright and still. Below me, the stairs fell steeply to the tessellated entrance hall. To my right the passage narrowed to the door behind which Mademoiselle Fournier slept, her wig upon a candlestick, her book and her spectacles lying on the rug at her side – so Marie had described her to me. Before me the stairs rose to the turn of the landing, from which a further flight led to the second floor, the third floor and the attics. The wall above the stair rail was white with the moon.

I felt the terror creeping up beneath my calm, though only as one might feel the shadow of pain while in the grip of a drug. I was waiting now as I had been instructed to wait, and I knew for what. I stared upwards, my gaze fastened upon the turn of the stairs.

Then, upon the moonlit wall, there appeared the shadow of a cone.

She stood just out of sight, her fools-capped head nodding forward, listening even as I was listening.

I held my breath. My forehead was ice-cold.

She came into view then, stepping carefully, one hand upholding a corner of her skirt, the other feeling its way along the wall. As she reached me I closed my eyes. I felt her pass by, knew she had gone along the passage to the room of Mademoiselle Fournier. I heard a door quietly opened and shut.

In those last moments of waiting my fear left me, though I could move neither hand nor foot. My ears were sharp for the least sound.

It came: a low and awful cry, tearing through the quiet of the house and blackening the moonlight itself. The door opened again.

She came hastening out, and in the shadow of the cap she smiled. She ran on tiptoe past me, up the stairs.

The last sound? I thought it had been the death cry of Mademoiselle Fournier; but there was yet another.

As Marie and the housekeeper came racing down, white-faced, from their rooms (they must have passed her as she stood in the shade) I heard very distinctly the piping voice of a young girl:

'*Tiens, Mademoiselle, je vous remercie beaucoup!*'

We went together, Marie, the housekeeper and I, into the room of Charlotte Fournier, and only I did not cry out when we looked upon the face.

'You see,' said Monsieur Oury, on the day I left Bellançay for ever to join my parents in Paris, 'she did make you her *confidante*. She gave to you the privilege of telling her story and publishing her revenge. Are you afraid of her now, knowing that there was no harm in her for *you*, knowing that she has gone for ever, to trouble no house again?'

'I am not afraid,' I said, and I believed it was true; but even now I cannot endure to awaken suddenly on moonlit nights, and I fling my arms about my husband and beg him to rouse up and speak with me until the dawn.

Brig-o-Dread

George Mackay Brown

When thou from hence away art past
Every nighte and alle
To Whinny-muir thou com'st at last
And Christe receive thy saule

From Whinny-muir when thou may'st pass
Every nighte and alle
To Brig-o-Dread thou com'st at last
And Christe receive thy saule

From Brig-o-Dread when thou may'st pass
Every nighte and alle
To Purgatory fire thou com'st at last
And Christe receive thy saule

'I should say at once who I am, in case it is necessary for me
to make a statement soon. My name is Arkol Andersvik. I
have been married for twelve years to my dear good wife
Freya. We have a son, aged eleven, called Thord, a clever
fair-haired boy whose craze, at the moment, is science fiction.
His school reports are promising – I will say no more. We live
in a fine old house in Hamnavoe, and I have a garden that
slopes down from the hill to the street. My shop is in the town
centre. Out of whalebone we – my brother and I – carve
souvenirs and mementos, and I deal in a variety of sealskin
articles. We do a fair business in summer, when the islands
are filled with tourists. I am a councillor. I am fifty years old.

'I try not to neglect the cultural side. For the past ten years
I have imposed a discipline on myself. I have striven to

acquaint myself with the best that has been sung and thought and written. You might call it a quest for truth and beauty. At the moment I am engaged on reading *Hamlet* for the third time. A poem that I chanced on last week really delighted me – the *Ode on a Grecian Urn* by Keats. It gave me a feeling of great purity and peace.

'My brother says this pursuit of culture is a substitute for the kirk pew. He may be right. I am not a religious man.

'Something strange has happened to me. That is why I am preparing this statement. I am not at home, nor in the shop. I don't know where I am, that's the truth. I am sitting on a bench in a bare room, like a prison cell. (But that is impossible.) Or it could be like a room where witnesses wait until they are called to give their evidence. It is worrying. I have never been involved in any kind of legal process. I intend to get to the bottom of it. It is a waste of my time, to put it mildly. I have a business to attend to. I have council work to see to this very evening. Freya will be very worried indeed.

'I have just discovered, with a certain relief, that I am not in prison; they have not removed my tie and bootlaces. I will go on writing in my notebook. That might help to clarify the situation in my mind.

'Wistan and I went seal-shooting yesterday afternoon, it being early closing day in the town. (Wistan is my younger brother.) We took our guns and motored four miles along the coast to a certain skerry where the seals come and go all summer. Some people wax sentimental over these animals. They invoke all the old legends about the selkie folk, half man and half seal, and their fondness for music. They denounce those who slaughter them, forgetting that they are voracious beasts that eat half the fish in the sea. The legends are charming, but most of that kind of talk is slush. Every man has his living to make. (What about the beasts that are slaughtered for our Sunday joints?)

'Wistan and I got out of the van at the cliff top and, carrying our guns, made our way carefully down salt broken ledges to the sea, only to find that the skerry was bare. The seals were away at their fishing. That was disappointing. We decided to wait for an hour or so, seeing that it was a fine afternoon and still early. I laid my gun along a ledge of rock. Wistan said he would take a walk round the coast, to see if he could find some shells or stones that − properly decorated − might tempt the tourists in search of souvenirs. He offered me his whisky flask. I declined, of course.

'A word or two about Wistan. He helps me in the business. I might have made him a partner but the truth is that there is a certain waywardness about him, an unreliability. He went to sea as a lad − came home after two years. My father used his influence to get Wistan work in a lawyer's office in Kirkwall, but he left, saying he couldn't bear the thought of scribbling and copying all day and every day, maybe for the rest of his life. For the next year or two he was a ne'er-do-well, spending his mornings in the pub, his afternoons in the billiard hall. Most evenings he would take his flute to dances in this parish and that. Wistan's conduct clouded our father's last years − I am certain of that.

'In the end I employed him in the shop. What else could I do? He is my brother. I did not want to see him wasting his life entirely. Wistan has talents. No one can make more handsome sealskin bags and slippers than him, and the way he paints birds and flowers on stone is masterly. He, not I, is the whale-bone carver. I pay him twelve pounds a week. He has a small house on a pier and lives there alone. (In case somebody should say, "That is a poor wage to give a man", I reply, "That is all the business will stand. Give him more, he would simply squander it ..." Besides, who but myself would employ him?)

'Poor Wistan! He is not highly regarded in the community. He was a delightful child, but some kind of raffishness entered into him at adolescence. It has never left him − the dreams, the deviousness. He drinks too much. Freya does not like him. I inflict him on her all the same − I insist that he comes to dinner every Sunday. In that way I can be sure that he gets at least one good meal in the week. He lounges about in the house all Sunday afternoon while I retire upstairs to my books and gramophone records.

'I thought to myself, between the crag and the skerry, "How on earth can Wistan afford whisky, on his wage?" I am not a skinflint, I hope, and I have nothing against a dram in the evening – but to booze in the middle of a summer afternoon! So I shook my head at the offered whisky flask. Still holding his gun in the crook of his arm, Wistan took a sip or two.

'A sleek head broke the surface fifty years out. Large liquid eyes looked at the hunters. I whistled. Wistan whistled, farther off. The creature stirred and eddied towards us. "Come on, my beauty", I remember saying. The water was suddenly alive with seals. And that is all I remember, until I found myself an hour ago in this cell-like room.

'It is very strange. Where am I? Where is Wistan? Where is the seal, the shore, the gun?'

Mr Andersvik had no sooner closed his notebook than he saw that the door of the mysterious room now stood open. It was a summer day: there was blue sky and white clouds. He was free to go it seemed.

Outside a signpost pointed: TO THE MOOR.

The landscape was strange to Mr Andersvik. The moor stretched, a wine-red emptiness, from horizon to horizon. It was eerie, to say the least. 'Well,' he thought, 'I'm bound to meet somebody who can tell me the way to Hamnavoe.' Indeed, when he took the track that wound into the moor, he saw a few people, and they too, like the landscape, had a remote dreamlike quality. They moved like somnambulists. Every heathfarer was solitary, and did not appear to be going anywhere. The moor was a slow soundless dance of intersections and turnings. The faces were down-tilted and preoccupied. It was soon obvious that the moor-dwellers wanted nothing to do with Mr Andersvik. As soon as he tried to approach one or other of these lonely ones, to ask the direction, they held out preventive hands – they had nothing

to say to him, they did not want to hear anything that he had
to say to them. Mr Andersvik was a bit hurt to begin with at
these rebuffs. But after he had walked a mile or two a kind of
contentment crept through him. It was quite pleasant out here
on the moor. What contented Mr Andersvik particularly was
the account he had written in his notebook in the courtroom –
he had set it down defensively (as if he was actually going to
be charged with some offence) in order to put a good face on
things, to cover up certain shames and deficiencies in his life
that were, after all, his own concern. But here, on this moor,
the images and rhythms of his prose pleased him very much
indeed; he could savour them with extraordinary vividness in
the solitude and silence. The remembrance was all pleasant, a
flattering unction. He began the cycle of his life again – Freya
and love and the garden. Thord and promise, Wistan and
responsibility, the shop and sealskins and money, the council
and honour, the temple of culture where he was a regular
devoted worshipper ... The second round of meditation was if
anything sweeter than the first ... This delight, he thought,
might go on for a long time. He very much hoped that it
would.

Mr Andersvik discovered, by certain rocks and a certain
gorse bush in the moor, that he had drifted round in two wide
circles. He was learning to behave in the manner of the
moor-dwellers. He halted.

'This will never do,' said Mr Andersvik to himself,
breaking the lovely idyll. 'I must get back. These memories
are not entirely true, I'm afraid. I must open the shop. There
is this council meeting tonight.'

He turned. He strode on across the moor, frowning and
purposeful. He was aware that his ankles had been rather
badly scratched with gorse-thorns – he had not noticed the
pain till now.

One of the moor people loomed close, with a tranced
preoccupied face, drifting on, smiling, in a wide arc across the
path of Mr Andersvik.

'Please,' said Mr Andersvik. 'One moment. I'm wanting

to get to Hamnavoe. Could you tell me if I'm going in the right direction?'

'What's wrong with this place?' said the dancer on the moor. 'What greater happiness could there be than this solitude? If you leave the moor you'll never get back. Beware, man. Your journey will end in ashes and smoke' ... The man drifted on, smiling, feeding deep on the honey of his past.

A finger of fear touched Mr Andersvik. To go on like that for ever, nourished on delusions! He was sure of one thing now, he wanted to break out of these endless self-flattering circles. He hurried on. Gorse tore at his ankles. Once he fell in a blazing bush – his hands bled and burned. He picked himself up and went on. Clumps of gorse blossomed here and there on the moor – it was impossible to avoid them entirely. Freya would have to put some disinfectant on a multitude of scratches.

He came over a ridge and saw with relief that the track gave onto a road.

It was strange. Mr Andersvik thought he knew every road in the island, but he had never been on this particular one. He came after a mile or so to a crossroads. The signpost said: TO THE BRIDGE. He walked on. Soon familiar hills and waters came about him. He recognized Kringklafiold and the twin lochs with the prehistoric stone circle. And over there was the farm where his sister Anne had gone to live and toil when she married Jock Onness thirty years before. Alas, Anne had been dead for four years. That death had been a blow to Mr Andersvik; Anne was one of the few folk he had ever had affection for. He felt a pang as he looked at the widowed farm. Should he call in and have a word with old Jock? He thought, not today. The shop – souvenirs, sealskin – he was losing pounds. Besides, he did not feel in a mood to explain to the old man all the strange things that had happened to him. Jock was very deaf, and not too bright.

He walked on. Ahead was the little stone bridge that divides sea from loch, parish from parish. Under the triple arch salt water mingles with sweet water twice a day. A woman was standing at the hither end of the bridge. She beckoned to Mr

Andersvik. Her face was tranquil, as if a quiet flame had passed through it.

It was his sister Anne.

He tried to speak, but his mouth locked on the words.

'Arkol,' she said. 'I've been expecting you. You've been on the moor a long time.'

'An hour or two,' he whispered.

'Longer than that,' said the dead woman. 'Oh, much longer. Well done, Arkol, all the same. Only a few folk have the strength to tear themselves away from that moor.'

Mr Andersvik took his first dark taste of death.

'I had to come and meet you,' said Anne, 'before you cross the bridge. Otherwise the pain would be too sudden and terrible.'

The half-ghost understood nothing of this. Death, in his understanding was a three-day feast of grief, a slow graining and seepage among roots, the last lonely splendour of the skeleton — but all enacted within a realm of oblivion (except for a few fading fragrances in the memories of friends). An eternity of harps, or flames, had always seemed to Mr Andersvik an insult to the human intelligence.

He could not by any means accept his present situation. Yet here he was, in dialogue with a kindly riddling ghost.

'Arkol, you've chosen the truth,' said Anne. 'That's splendid. But the truth is cruel, Arkol. A poor naked truth-bound ghost has a terrible journey to go.'

'What happened to me?' said Mr Andersvik after a time.

'A gun-shot wound. In the head. The court said "Self-inflicted. Death by misadventure." Poor Arkol.'

'My gun was six yards away on a ledge of rock!' cried Mr Andersvik. 'That's impossible!'

'Poor Arkol,' she said again. 'But that's only the start. Are you willing to be dead?'

'No,' he cried. 'I don't believe it. Don't touch me. I can't be dead. I have years of work in front of me. Thord must be given a good start. Freya must be provided for. There's the housing committee and the graveyard committee. I am going to extend the business. I haven't made a will.'

His sister soothed him. She spoke to him with all the tenderness and kindness that in the old days had persuaded Mr Andersvik that, for example, he must really not be so pompous, he must learn to laugh at himself a little; that he must give Freya a more generous housekeeping allowance, she was having to pinch here and patch there – it was a shame, him with all that money and all these pretensions ... Now Mr Andersvik sensed a new depth in his sister's concern. He bowed his head. He yielded to her wisdom, there on the bridge between the dead and the living. Anne kissed him on the mouth, and so sealed his death for him.

Arkol crossed over the bridge then.

In darkness the dead man returned to the dimension he had left. Time is a slow banked smoulder to the living. To the dead it is an august merciless ordering of flames, in which the tormented one must learn at last to be a dancer.

His fellow-councillors were sitting in the council chamber. There was a new member seated in the chair he normally occupied – his brother Wistan. The provost was making some kind of formal speech ... 'welcome our new councillor, Mr Wistan Andersvik, to this chamber. We welcome him doubly in that he is the brother of the late councillor Arkol Andersvik, who died in such tragic circumstances a month ago. The late councillor was a highly valued member of this assembly. His wisdom and his humanity will be greatly missed. Some said that maybe he was over-cautious in this matter and that, but my reply to that was always, "Arkol Andersvik is a true custodian of the public purse" ... A more prudent man never walked the streets of this burgh. We trust, indeed we know, that his brother will be in all respects a worthy successor. He will bring imagination to our debates where the lamented elder brother gave us abundant practical sense. I will ask you, fellow-councillors, to be upstanding for one minute as a token of our respect for that good man who was taken so suddenly from our midst....'

They stood there, a lugubrious circle, and Wistan stood

among them. Arkol felt for the first time the pain of the wound in his head. He cried out that they had taken a murderer into their fold, a brother-killer, but no one heard him. They passed onto the next business on the agenda....

Arkol shook himself clear of that flame. Darkness beset him again for a while (he did not know how long); then, far on, a new flame summoned a white splash of time. He eddied like a moth towards it ... What shuttered place was he standing in? Light sifted through slatted window blinds, and of course he soon recognized it: it was his shop. The clock ticked on the shelf, spilling busy seconds into his timelessness. It was a quarter past ten in the morning, and still the door hadn't been opened to the public. So, it had come to this. How had Freya ever allowed it! She ought to have sold the business as a going concern. It had been a small gold-mine. Plenty of folk would have given a handsome price for 'A. Andersvik – Novelties, Presents, and Souvenirs'.

The key shrieked in the lock. The street-door opened. A familiar shadow stood there carrying a heavy bucket.

Arkol saw in the new light from the street that there were no longer any painted pebbles or sealskin on the shelves. In their place were pieces of baked hollowed-out clay, garishly decorated. So Wistan had set himself up as a potter? The shop was a shambles – it reeked of burnt earth.

'You killed me,' he said sternly. 'But you're too loutish and lazy to enjoy the fruits of murder. How dare you ruin a good business! Filthying my shop with your mud and fire!'

Wistan set his bucket of clay beside the warm kiln. He moved over to the bench. He began to knead a lump of clay with knuckles and fingers. He was humming happily to himself ....

Arkol came out of the flame singed and trembling.

He stood on Celia's pier in the first light of morning. (Time here was, as always, surely, a limpid invisible burning.) The old women arrived with their cats and basins while the fishermen (just back from the west) handed up the steps baskets of haddock. It was a famous place for gossip and opinion and elegy. Gulls, savage naked hungers, wheeled between the boat and the pier.

They were speaking about a death.

'Accident,' Maisie Ness was saying. 'That makes me laugh. You can't shoot yourself by accident. He was in trouble, if you ask me. He was on the verge of bankruptcy. So I heard. There was nothing else for him to do but shoot himself.'

'Well,' said Andrina Moar, 'he isn't that much of a miss. The swank of him! The strut of the creature along the street!'

Not one face on Celia's pier stilled with sorrow for the dead man. Instead the women, old and young, began to tear at Arkol's death like gulls among fish guts.

The haddocks gulped and shrugged in their baskets: dying gleams. Cats mewed. Sea and sky and stone was an asylum of gulls. The voices went on and on in the sunlight....

The darkness wrapped him away, trembling, from the slanders of the living.

He emerged into fragrance and sweetness. A peaceful green rectangle sloped down from the hill to the clustered roofs of Hamnavoe: his garden. What man was that sitting on the bench under the sycamore tree? It was, again, Wistan. Years had passed. Wistan's face was thin and sick and grey. Was he perhaps on the point of accomplishing his suicide by alcohol (an end that Arkol had more than once prophesied)? Then Arkol saw that Wistan was somehow injured – his right hand (the one that had pulled the trigger) was white and thick with bandaging. Wistan looked very seedy indeed in that net of green wavering shadows. (So Freya, out of the foolish kindness of her heart, had taken the creature into her house, for cure or for death.)

Freya came out of the kitchen into the sunlight. There was an extra decade of flesh and capability on her now. She was carrying a tray with salves and bandages on it. Wistan looked up. Blackbirds sang here and there in the bushes. It was a marvellous summer morning. The man and the woman smiled at each other. But immediately the shadow fell on Wistan's face again.

Freya set down the tray on the bench. She bent forward and kissed him on the forehead.

The ghost stirred in its flame.

'So, dearest,' said Freya, 'this is one of your black days, is it?' ... She knelt on the grass and began to undo the bandage on Wistan's hand.

There was a passionate outpouring of song from the rosebush at the bottom of the lawn.

'It *was* an accident,' said Wistan in the shivering silence that followed. 'The gun went off in my hands. But, dear, he'd done such terrible things, anything he could think of – you know – to make me eat dirt, that sometimes I think ...'

'We've been through all that before,' said Freya the comforter. 'I know. You've told me hundreds of times ...' She kissed the scarred hand. 'There, if it helps you. Of course it was an accident. Just as you didn't mean to put your hand in the kiln last Friday. You were aiming for the seal. You might as well argue that *I* killed Arkol. If I didn't particularly want him to die, that was just because I'd got used to him. I realize that now ... You wedged the gun into his arms – that's all you have to reproach yourself with, love. It was nothing. It was clever of you, in fact. It saved a lot of trouble, a lot of fuss and anger and suspicion.'

Wistan closed his eyes. Freya began to spread the unguent over his charred palm.

Freya said, after another blackbird interlude, 'I don't think now, looking back, that I ever really liked Arkol. The meanness of him, the arrogance! That horrible flesh lying beside me all night and every night! But you, dear, the first time I ever saw you....'

The ghost smouldered in the garden, among the sievings of birdsong. It glowed. It reeked. It longed to be anywhere, in any darkness, away from this incestuous place. Then it remembered, and acquiesced in the stake. The flames thickened. The ghost burned terribly. Yet it forced itself to look while Freya wrapped Wistan's wound in new bandages, swiftly, delicately, tenderly; and even afterwards, when the man and the woman enfolded each other on the long bench.

If only a ghost could die ... It bore into the darkness terrible new scorchings.

Arkol came to a room that had a stale smell in it. It was the study where he had sought to improve his mind with good music and books. A reproduction of Van Gogh's *Sunflowers* hung over the mantelpiece. Freya, it seemed, had sealed the place off like a mausoleum. The dust whispered to him from shelf and record-player, 'What good was it to you, after all? You went through life blind and dense and hoodwinked. Here we are, Chopin and Jane Austen and Shelley, and we tried to tell you many a wise and many a true thing, but it only served to bolster your self-importance. Go and look for some peace now, poor ghost, if you can ...' No one entered the study. *Hamlet* was lying on the table, just as he had left it the day before his murder, and *The Oxford Book of English Verse*, open at 'The Grecian Urn'. The ghost bent over the grey page. The poem was, as never before, a cold pure round of silence; a fold; a chalice for the transmutation of all sublunary vanities and grief.

But that solace was not for him. New flames – white splashings of time – summoned him. He was as hungry as a moth now for the anguish and the healing.

Arkol passed deeper into the charred ruins of his life. In another room a youth was sitting at a table, making notes of some kind. Thord had grown into a pleasant-looking young man. Bits of *Hamlet* drifted through the ghost: 'Thy father's spirit ...' 'He took me grossly full of bread ...' 'Avenge his foul and most unnatural murder ...' The ghost smiled, in spite of its pain. As if this ordinary youth could ever be roused to such eagle-heights of rage, assoilment, passion! What had Thord done with his life? Arkol had had high hopes of the shy eager boy with his pile of science fiction books on his bedside table. Thord, he had thought, might well become a physicist, or a writer, or even a seeker among the stars. The ghost bent over the warm shoulder. Thord was filling up a football pools coupon. On the door-hook hung a postman's cap. To this favour the clever little boy had come: knocking at doors with white squares of gossip, propaganda, trivia. It did not matter. The ghost drank the beauty of his son's face – and saw, without rage, how like his mother he was now. He longed to linger out his time in this flame. But, shadow by slow shadow, he was folded in oblivion once more....

This was the rock, right enough. Coldness and heaviness and poise lay across the ghost, a gun-shape. It oppressed him. He wished he were free of it. Another man was walking on the loose stones of the beach fifty yards away. The man stooped and picked up a stone or a shell every now and again. The man uncorked a flask and tilted it towards his mouth. A sleek head broke the grey surface – a seal, with large dark brimming eyes. The ghost whistled, but no smallest sound was added to the wash of the waves, the sliding of stones, the click of a bolt. There was another louder whistle farther along the shore. Suddenly the bay was musical with seals; they clustered about the off-shore rock; their sea-dance was over, they clambered awkwardly on to the stone. 'Come on, my beauties ...' Whitman's song came on the wind:

I think I could turn and live with animals,
They are so placid and self-contained.

A line of Coleridge flowered: 'he blessed them in his heart ...' The ghost raised an invisible hand seaward. He greeted the clean swift beautiful creatures of the ocean. He acknowledged the long wars of man against that innocent kingdom. He whispered for forgiveness. Then he turned calmly to face the blaze and the roar.

The day began with streams of blood. All the village followed the white-robed priest and the heifer whose horns were hidden under wreaths and clusters of blossom. Children danced and shouted. The throng of people disappeared beyond the last house of the village.

The only man who did not go to the ceremony sat in his cell and waited. The door had been open since first light.

He heard, after a long loaded silence, a whisper on the hillside, a fierce flailing of hooves, a surge and a spattering; then a wild ecstatic cry.

Presently the folk returned to the village. The lonely celebrant went with his red arms into a small house at the shore. The village street was soon empty. Family by family, purified, was eating its morning meal.

Not long afterwards the prisoner was summoned out to the village square.

A court of some kind was assembled and waiting. The square brimmed like a well with light. People of all ages sat here and there. Arkol was invited to station himself beside a sun-warmed stone.

The interrogator faced Arkol. Four people sat apart from the others, against the wall of the pottery-maker. Arkol took them to be a panel of judges. They consulted together. Occasionally one looked across at him and smiled.

The interrogator began with a reading out of the statement that Arkol had originally made: 'trust of the townsfolk ...' 'quest for truth and beauty ...' 'intend to get to the bottom of this ...' The interrogator was interrupted every now and again by wondering laughter.

The older men and women sat in their doorsteps. Children – hidden voices – shouted in the gardens behind the street. The sound of the sea was everywhere. A young man went round the people in the square carrying a tray with a pitcher and tankards. An old man nodded approval over the white blown fleece of foam. An old woman shook her head reprovingly at all the raised tankards.

The voice of the interrogator – austere, measured, and melodious – reached into the bright morning. The villagers were rather bored with the proceedings, on the whole. Arkol could tell by their faces that they would much rather have been down at the fishing boats, or on the hill with their sheep, than wasting the day with such a trivial case. But at the end, he supposed, the villagers would have to give some kind of a verdict in the square.

Some young folk had got out of it by bathing. Arkol could hear shouts along the beach and the splash of bodies in the surf. There were mocking harp-like cries, then a sudden silence. A young man, naked and gleaming with sun and water, passed hurriedly through the square and entered a small steep alley. Children shrieked at the sea drops that shivered and showered over them. Voices from the rocks called for the insulted one to come back. A girl with wet hair appeared at the mouth of a seaward close. 'We're sorry, Adon,' she called. 'Please come back. Please.'

'Silence,' said the interrogator sternly. 'Go back to the sea. We are considering an important application.'

The girl withdrew bright hair, bright shoulders.

The case suffered no more interruptions. The interrogator paused upon this phrase and that: ... 'A word or two about Wistan ...' 'I am not a skinflint, I hope'. An old man laughed above his ale. Arkol smiled ruefully.

A boy called from a hidden garden that he had caught a butterfly – he had – but it had wriggled out of his fingers and was free in the wind once more.

What intrigued Arkol more than anything that morning were the faces of the four judges who, he supposed, would finally decide whether his application should be granted or no. They sat on a long bench in front of the interrogator. It was as if old woodcuts and frontispieces and dead music had trembled and quickened. These were the jurors: a man with wild hair and a wild mouth – a young woman who in spite of merry mischievous eyes looked rather prim – a man with a russet beard and a scar at one ear – long lank hair over a lank dark cheek, a velvet jacket, lank fingers: the hollows and shadows scattered whenever the man smiled, which was often.

There was silence in the square. The reading of the statement was over.

The cup-bearer had spread a white cloth on a long trestle table. He reappeared in the square now, carrying a tray with steaming fish on it, and bread. He began to arrange seats.

'The statement, it is a tissue of lies,' said the hollow-cheeked juror in a foreign accent. All the jurors nodded. They looked at Arkol and smiled.

'The wonder is how he ever managed to escape,' said Van Gogh. 'I took him for a typical moor-dweller as soon as he arrived here last night.'

'He is a hero,' said a girl in a doorway who was feeding a baby at her breast.

The bathers came up from the sea. The girl whose face had been glimpsed for a moment between the houses looked anxious now. Her companions tried to reassure her. They went in an agitated troop up one of the alleys.

The cup-bearer carried from the inn a huge pitcher − both his arms were round it − some wine slurped over onto the cobblestones. An old man cried out in alarm. But the pitcher was safely deposited at last among the fish and the bread.

'As one of the villagers,' said a man who was leaning against a wall smoking a pipe, 'I think he must at least do this before we give him the stones to build a house − he must alter the account of his life so that it comes a bit nearer the truth.'

The villagers shouted their approval.

'You can't eat or drink with us, you understand,' said the interrogator to Arkol, 'or stay here in this village, until you have paid your debt to the truth. You must revise your statement in certain respects. You will be given pen and paper. Now that you've been through the fire, I think you may enjoy doing it.'

The villagers turned away from Arkol. They began to gather round the table. The bathers, all but two, came down the alley and joined the others. Mugs and pieces of bread were passed round − there was a mingling of courtesy and banter. Three seats were empty.

Arkol sat on a sunlit step. He poised his pen over the paper. He wondered how to begin.

The children's voices drifted down from the hillside. They were filling baskets with blackberries. Pure echoes fell into the square. The children shouted that they would not be home till sunset.

The lovers who had quarrelled on the sea verge stood in the mouth of the close. They were tranquil and smiling now. They moved into sunlight. Folk rose up at the table to let them pass on to their places.

Arkol wrote. Phrases with some beauty and truth in them began to come, with difficulty. He longed to sit among the villagers, and share their meal. But the feast was eternal. He hoped that he might be able, before it was over, to present to the elders the poem of his life.

Thus I Refute Beelzy

John Collier

'There goes the tea bell,' said Mrs Carter. 'I hope Simon hears it.'

They looked out from the window of the drawing room. The long garden, agreeably neglected, ended in a waste plot. Here a little summerhouse was passing close by beauty on its way to complete decay. This was Simon's retreat. It was almost completely screened by the tangled branches of the apple tree and the pear tree, planted too close together, as they always are in suburban gardens. They caught a glimpse of him now and then, as he strutted up and down, mouthing and gesticulating, performing all the solemn mumbo jumbo of small boys who spend long afternoons at the forgotten ends of long gardens.

'There he is, bless him,' said Betty.

'Playing his game,' said Mrs Carter. 'He won't play with the other children any more. And if I go down there – the temper! And comes in tired out.'

'He doesn't have his sleep in the afternoons?' asked Betty.

'You know what Big Simon's ideas are,' said Mrs Carter. ' "Let him choose for himself," he says. That's what he chooses, and he comes in as white as a sheet.'

'Look. He's heard the bell,' said Betty. The expression was justified, though the bell had ceased ringing a full minute ago. Small Simon stopped in his parade exactly as if its tinny dingle had at that moment reached his ear. They watched him perform certain ritual sweeps and scratchings with his little stick, and come lagging over the hot and flaggy grass towards the house.

Mrs Carter led the way down to the playroom, or garden-room, which was also the tearoom for hot days. It had been the huge scullery of this tall Georgian house. Now the walls were cream-washed, there was coarse blue net in the windows, canvas-covered armchairs on the stone floor, and a reproduction of Van Gogh's *Sunflowers* over the mantelpiece.

Small Simon came drifting in, and accorded Betty a perfunctory greeting. His face was an almost perfect triangle, pointed at the chin, and he was paler than he should have been. 'The little elf-child!' cried Betty.

Simon looked at her. 'No,' said he.

At that moment the door opened, and Mr Carter came in, rubbing his hands. He was a dentist, and washed them before and after everything he did. 'You!' said his wife. 'Home already!'

'Not unwelcome, I hope,' said Mr Carter, nodding to Betty. 'Two people cancelled their appointments; I decided to come home. I said, I hope I am not unwelcome.'

'Silly!' said his wife. 'Of course not.'

'Small Simon seems doubtful,' continued Mr Carter. 'Small Simon, are you sorry to see me at tea with you?'

'No, Daddy.'

'No, what?'

'No, Big Simon.'

'That's right. Big Simon and Small Simon. That sounds more like friends, doesn't it? At one time little boys had to call their father "sir". If they forgot — a good spanking. On the bottom, Small Simon! On the bottom!' said Mr Carter, washing his hands once more with his invisible soap and water.

The little boy turned crimson with shame or rage.

'But now, you see,' said Betty, to help, 'you can call your father whatever you like.'

'And what,' asked Mr Carter, 'has Small Simon been doing this afternoon? While Big Simon has been at work.'

'Nothing,' muttered his son.

'Then you have been bored,' said Mr Carter, 'Learn from

experience, Small Simon. Tomorrow, do something amusing, and you will not be bored. I want him to learn from experience, Betty. That is my way, the *new* way.'

'I have learned,' said the boy, speaking like an old, tired man, as little boys so often do.

'It would hardly seem so,' said Mr Carter, 'if you sit on your behind all the afternoon, doing nothing. Had *my* father caught me doing nothing, I should not have sat very comfortably.'

'He played,' said Mrs Carter.

'A bit,' said the boy, shifting on his chair.

'Too much,' said Mrs Carter. 'He comes in all nervy and dazed. He ought to have his rest.'

'He is six,' said her husband. 'He is a reasonable being. He must choose for himself. But what game is this, Small Simon, that is worth getting nervy and dazed over? There are very few games as good as all that.'

'It's nothing,' said the boy.

'Oh, come,' said his father. 'We are friends, are we not? You can tell me. I was a Small Simon once, just like you, and played the same games you play. Of course there were no airplanes in those days. With whom do you play this fine game? Come on, we must all answer civil questions, or the world would never go round. With whom do you play?'

'Mr Beelzy,' said the boy, unable to resist.

'Mr Beelzy?' said his father, raising his eyebrows inquiringly at his wife.

'It's a game he makes up,' said she.

'Not makes up!' cried the boy. 'Fool!'

'That is telling stories,' said his mother. 'And rude as well. We had better talk of something different.'

'No wonder he is rude,' said Mr Carter, 'if you say he tells lies, and then insist on changing the subject. He tells you his fantasy: you implant a guilt feeling. What can you expect? A defence mechanism. Then you get a real lie.'

'Like in *These Three*,' said Betty. 'Only different, of course. *She* was an unblushing little liar.'

'I would have made her blush,' said Mr Carter, 'in the proper part of her anatomy. But Small Simon is in the fantasy stage. Are you not, Small Simon? You just make things up.'

'No, I don't,' said the boy.

'You do,' said his father. 'And because you do, it is not too late to reason with you. There is no harm in a fantasy, old chap. There is no harm in a bit of make-believe. Only you have to know the difference between daydreams and real things, or your brain will never grow. It will never be the brain of a Big Simon. So come on. Let us hear about this Mr Beelzy of yours. Come on. What is he like?'

'He isn't like anything,' said the boy.

'Like nothing on earth?' said his father. 'That's a terrible fellow.'

'I'm not frightened of him,' said the child, smiling. 'Not a bit.'

'I should hope not,' said his father. 'If you were, you would be frightening yourself. I am always telling people, older people than you are, that they are just frightening themselves. Is he a funny man? Is he a giant?'

'Sometimes he is,' said the little boy.

'Sometimes one thing, sometimes another,' said his father. 'Sounds pretty vague. Why can't you tell us just what he's like?'

'I love him,' said the small boy. 'He loves me.'

'That's a big word,' said Mr Carter. 'That might be better kept for real things, like Big Simon and Small Simon.'

'He is real,' said the boy, passionately. 'He's not a fool. He's real.'

'Listen,' said his father. 'When you go down the garden there's nobody there. Is there?'

'No,' said the boy.

'Then you think of him, inside your head, and he comes.'

'No,' said Small Simon. 'I have to do something with my stick.'

'That doesn't matter.'

'Yes, it does.'

'Small Simon, you are being obstinate,' said Mr Carter. 'I am trying to explain something to you. I have been longer in the world than you have, so naturally I am older and wiser. I am explaining that Mr Beelzy is a fantasy of yours. Do you hear? Do you understand?'

'Yes, Daddy.'

'He is a game. He is a let's-pretend.'

The little boy looked down at his plate, smiling resignedly.

'I hope you are listening to me,' said his father. 'All you have to do is to say, "I have been playing a game of let's-pretend. With someone I make up, called Mr Beelzy." Then no one will say you tell lies, and you will know the difference between dreams and reality. Mr Beelzy is a daydream.'

The little boy still stared at his plate.

'He is sometimes there and sometimes not there,' pursued Mr Carter. 'Sometimes he's like one thing, sometimes another. You can't really see him. Not as you see me, I am real. You can't touch him. You can touch me. I can touch you.' Mr Carter stretched out his big, white, dentist's hand, and took his little son by the shoulder. He stopped speaking for a moment and tightened his hand. The little boy sank his head still lower.

'Now you know the difference,' said Mr Carter, 'between a pretend and a real thing. You and I are one thing; he is another. Which is the pretend? Come on. Answer me. Which is the pretend?'

'Big Simon and Small Simon,' said the little boy.

'Don't!' cried Betty, and at once put her hand over her mouth, for why should a visitor cry 'Don't!' when a father is explaining things in a scientific and modern way?

'Well, my boy,' said Mr Carter, 'I have said you must be allowed to learn from experience. Go upstairs. Right up to your room. You shall learn whether it is better to reason, or to be perverse and obstinate. Go up. I shall follow you.'

'You are not going to beat the child?' cried Mrs Carter.

'No,' said the little boy. 'Mr Beelzy won't let him.'

'Go on up with you!' shouted his father.

Small Simon stopped at the door. 'He said he wouldn't let anyone hurt me,' he whimpered. 'He said he'd come like a lion, with wings on, and eat them up.'

'You'll learn how real he is!' shouted his father after him. 'If you can't learn it at one end, you shall learn it at the other. I'll have your breeches down. I shall finish my cup of tea first, however,' said he to the two women.

Neither of them spoke. Mr Carter finished his tea, and unhurriedly left the room, washing his hands with his invisible soap and water.

Mrs Carter said nothing. Betty could think of nothing to say. She wanted to be talking: she was afraid of what they might hear.

Suddenly it came. It seemed to tear the air apart. 'Good God!' she cried. 'What was that? He's hurt him.' She sprang out of her chair, her silly eyes flashing behind her glasses. 'I'm going up there!' she cried, trembling.

'Yes, let us go up,' said Mrs Carter. 'Let us go up. That was not Small Simon.'

It was on the second-floor landing that they found the shoe, with the man's foot still in it, like that last morsel of a mouse which sometimes falls from the jaws of a hasty cat.

Royal Jelly

Roald Dahl

'It worries me to death, Albert, it really does,' Mrs Taylor said.

She kept her eyes fixed on the baby who was now lying absolutely motionless in the crook of her left arm.

'I just know there's something wrong.'

The skin on the baby's face had a pearly translucent quality and was stretched very tightly over the bones.

'Try again,' Albert Taylor said.

'It won't do any good.'

'You have to keep trying, Mabel,' he said.

She lifted the bottle out of the saucepan of hot water and shook a few drops of milk on to the inside of her wrist, testing for temperature.

'Come on,' she whispered. 'Come on, my baby. Wake up and take a bit more of this.'

There was a small lamp on the table close by that made a soft yellow glow all around her.

'Please,' she said. 'Take just a weeny bit more.'

The husband watched her over the top of his magazine. She was half dead with exhaustion, he could see that, and the pale oval face, usually so grave and serene, had taken on a kind of pinched and desperate look. But even so, the drop of her head as she gazed down at the child was curiously beautiful.

'You see,' she murmured. 'It's no good. She won't have it.'

She held the bottle up to the light, squinting at the calibrations.

'One ounce again. That's all she's taken. No – it isn't even that. It's only three-quarters. It's not enough to keep body and soul together, Albert, it really isn't. It worries me to death.'

'I know,' he said.

'If only they could *find out* what was wrong.'

'There's nothing wrong, Mabel. It's just a matter of time.'

'Of course there's something wrong.'

'Dr Robinson says no.'

'Look,' she said, standing up. 'You can't tell me it's natural for a six-weeks-old child to weigh less, less by more than *two whole pounds* than she did when she was born! Just look at those legs! They're nothing but skin and bone!'

The tiny baby lay limply on her arm, not moving.

'Dr Robinson said you was to stop worrying, Mabel. So did that other one.'

'Ha!' she said. 'Isn't that wonderful! I'm to stop worrying!'

'Now, Mabel.'

'What does he want me to do? Treat it as some sort of a joke?'

'He didn't say that.'

'I hate doctors! I hate them all!' she cried, and she swung away from him and walked quickly out of the room towards the stairs, carrying the baby with her.

Albert Taylor stayed where he was and let her go.

In a little while he heard her moving about in the bedroom directly over his head, quick nervous footsteps going tap tap tap on the linoleum above. Soon the footsteps would stop, and then he would have to get up and follow her, and when he went into the bedroom he would find her sitting beside the cot as usual, staring at the child and crying softly to herself and refusing to move.

'She's starving, Albert,' she would say.

'Of course she's not starving.'

'She *is* starving. I know she is. And Albert?'

'Yes?'

'I believe you know it too, but you won't admit it. Isn't that right?'

Every night now it was like this.

Last week they had taken the child back to the hospital, and the doctor had examined it carefully and told them that there was nothing the matter.

'It took us nine years to get this baby, Doctor,' Mabel had said. 'I think it would kill me if anything should happen to her.'

That was six days ago and since then it had lost another five ounces.

But worrying about it wasn't going to help anybody, Albert Taylor told himself. One simply had to trust the doctor on a thing like this. He picked up the magazine that was still lying on his lap and glanced idly down the list of contents to see what it had to offer this week:

Among the Bees in May
Honey Cookery
The Bee Farmer and the B. Pharm.
Experiences in the Control of Nosema
The Latest on Royal Jelly
This Week in the Apiary
The Healing Power of Propolis
Regurgitations
British Beekeepers Annual Dinner
Association News

All his life Albert Taylor had been fascinated by anything that had to do with bees. As a small boy he used often to catch them in his bare hands and go running with them into the house to show to his mother, and sometimes he would put them on his face and let them crawl about over his cheeks and neck, and the astonishing thing about it all was that he never got stung. On the contrary, the bees seemed to enjoy being with him. They never tried to fly away, and to get rid of them he would have to brush them off gently with his fingers. Even then they would frequently return and settle again on his arm or hand or knee, any place where the skin was bare.

His father, who was a bricklayer, said there must be some witch's stench about the boy, something noxious that came oozing out through the pores of the skin, and that no good would ever come of it, hypnotizing insects like that. But the mother said it was a gift given him by God, and even went so far as to compare him with St Francis and the birds.

As he grew older, Albert Taylor's fascination with bees developed into an obsession, and by the time he was twelve he had built his first hive. The following summer he had captured his first swarm. Two years later, at the age of fourteen, he had no less than five hives standing neatly in a row against the fence in his father's small back yard, and already – apart from the normal task of producing honey – he was practising the delicate and complicated business of rearing his own queens, grafting larvae into artificial cell cups, and all the rest of it.

He never had to use smoke when there was work to do inside a hive, and he never wore gloves on his hands or a net over his head. Clearly there was some strange sympathy between this boy and the bees, and down in the village, in the shops and pubs, they began to speak about him with a certain kind of respect, and people started coming up to the house to buy his honey.

When he was eighteen, he had rented one acre of rough pasture alongside a cherry orchard down the valley about a mile from the village, and there he had set out to establish his own business. Now, eleven years later, he was still in the same spot, but he had six acres of ground instead of one, two hundred and forty well-stocked hives, and a small house that he'd built mainly with his own hands. He had married at the age of twenty and that, apart from the fact that it had taken them over nine years to get a child, had also been a success. In fact, everything had gone pretty well for Albert until this strange little baby girl came along and started frightening them out of their wits by refusing to eat properly and losing weight every day.

He looked up from the magazine and began thinking about his daughter.

That evening, for instance, when she had opened her eyes at the beginning of the feed, he had gazed into them and seen something that frightened him to death — a kind of misty vacant stare, as though the eyes themselves were not connected to the brain at all but were just lying loose in their sockets like a couple of small grey marbles.

Did those doctors really know what they were talking about?

He reached for an ashtray and started slowly picking the ashes out from the bowl of his pipe with a matchstick.

One could always take her along to another hospital, somewhere in Oxford perhaps. He might suggest that to Mabel when he went upstairs.

He could still hear her moving around in the bedroom, but she must have taken off her shoes now and put on slippers because the noise was very faint.

He switched his attention back to the magazine and went on with his reading. He finished the article called 'Experiences in the Control of Nosema', then turned over the page and began reading the next one, 'The Latest on Royal Jelly'. He doubted very much whether there would be anything in this that he didn't know already:

What is this wonderful substance called royal jelly?

He reached for the tin of tobacco on the table beside him and began filling his pipe, still reading.

Royal jelly is a glandular secretion produced by the nurse bees to feed the larvae immediately they have hatched from the egg. The pharyngeal glands of bees produce this substance in much the same way as the mammary glands of vertebrates produce milk. The fact is of great biological interest because no other insects in the world are known to have evolved such a process.

All old stuff, he told himself, but for want of anything better to do, he continued to read.

Royal jelly is fed in concentrated form to all bee larvae for the first three days after hatching from the egg; but beyond

III

that point, for all those who are destined to become drones or workers, this precious food is greatly diluted with honey and pollen. On the other hand, the larvae which are destined to become queens are fed throughout the whole of their larval period on a concentrated diet of pure royal jelly. Hence the name.

Above him, up in the bedroom, the noise of the footsteps had stopped altogether. The house was quiet. He struck a match and put it to his pipe.

Royal jelly must be a substance of tremendous nourishing power, for on this diet alone, the honey-bee larva increases in weight fifteen hundred times in five days.

That was probably about right, he thought, although for some reason it had never occurred to him to consider larval growth in terms of weight before.

This is as if a seven-and-a-half-pound baby should increase in that time to five tons.

Albert Taylor stopped and read that sentence again.
He read it a third time.

This is as if a seven-and-a-half-pound baby ...

'Mabel!' he cried, jumping up from his chair. 'Mabel! Come here!'
He went out into the hall and stood at the foot of the stairs calling for her to come down.
There was no answer.
He ran up the stairs and switched on the light on the landing. The bedroom door was closed. He crossed the landing and opened it and stood in the doorway looking into the dark room. 'Mabel,' he said. 'Come downstairs a moment, will you please? I've just had a bit of an idea. It's about the baby.'
The light from the landing behind him cast a faint glow over the bed and he could see her dimly now, lying on her

stomach with her face buried in the pillow and her arms up over her head. She was crying again.

'Mabel,' he said, going over to her, touching her shoulder. 'Please come down a moment. This may be important.'

'Go away,' she said. 'Leave me alone.'

'Don't you want to hear about my idea?'

'Oh, Albert, I'm *tired*,' she sobbed. 'I'm so tired I don't know what I'm doing any more. I don't think I can go on. I don't think I can stand it.'

There was a pause. Albert Taylor turned away from her and walked slowly over to the cradle where the baby was lying, and peered in. It was too dark for him to see the child's face, but when he bent down close he could hear the sound of breathing, very faint and quick. 'What time is the next feed?' he asked.

'Two o'clock, I suppose.'

'And the one after that?'

'Six in the morning.'

'I'll do them both,' he said. 'You go to sleep.'

She didn't answer.

'You get properly into bed, Mabel, and go straight to sleep, you understand? And stop worrying. I'm taking over completely for the next twelve hours. You'll give yourself a nervous breakdown going on like this.'

'Yes,' she said. 'I know.'

'I'm taking the nipper and myself *and* the alarm clock into the spare room this very moment, so you just lie down and relax and forget all about us. Right?' Already he was pushing the cradle out through the door.

'Oh, Albert,' she sobbed.

'Don't you worry about a thing. Leave it to me.'

'Albert ...'

'Yes?'

'I love you, Albert.'

'I love you too, Mabel. Now go to sleep.'

Albert Taylor didn't see his wife again until nearly eleven o'clock the next morning.

'Good *gracious* me!' she cried, rushing down the stairs in dressing-gown and slippers. 'Albert! Just look at the time! I must have slept twelve hours at least! Is everything all right? What happened?'

He was sitting quietly in his armchair, smoking a pipe and reading the morning paper. The baby was in a sort of carry-cot on the floor at his feet, sleeping.

'Hullo, dear,' he said, smiling.

She ran over to the cot and looked in. 'Did she take anything, Albert? How many times have you fed her? She was due for another one at ten o'clock, did you know that?'

Albert Taylor folded the newspaper neatly into a square and put it away on the side table. 'I fed her at two in the morning,' he said, 'and she took about half an ounce, no more. I fed her again at six and she did a bit better that time, two ounces....'

'*Two ounces!* Oh, Albert, that's marvellous!'

'And we just finished the last feed ten minutes ago. There's the bottle on the mantelpiece. Only one ounce left. She drank three. How's that?' He was grinning proudly, delighted with his achievement.

The woman quickly got down on her knees and peered at the baby.

'Don't she look better?' he asked eagerly. 'Don't she look fatter in the face?'

'It may sound silly,' the wife said, 'but I actually think she does. Oh, Albert, you're a marvel! How did you do it?'

'She's turning the corner,' he said. 'That's all it is. Just like the doctor prophesied, she's turning the corner.'

'I pray to God you're right, Albert.'

'Of course I'm right. From now on, you watch her go.'

The woman was gazing lovingly at the baby.

'You look a lot better yourself too, Mabel.'

'I feel wonderful. I'm sorry about last night.'

'Let's keep it this way,' he said. 'I'll do all the night feeds in future. You do the day ones.'

She looked up at him across the cot, frowning. 'No,' she

said. 'Oh no, I wouldn't allow you to do that.'

'I don't want you to have a breakdown, Mabel.'

'I won't, not now I've had some sleep.'

'Much better we share it.'

'No, Albert. This is my job and I intend to do it. Last night won't happen again.'

There was a pause. Albert Taylor took the pipe out of his mouth and examined the grain on the bowl. 'All right,' he said. 'In that case I'll just relieve you of the donkey work, I'll do all the sterilizing and the mixing of the food and getting everything ready. That'll help you a bit, anyway.'

She looked at him carefully, wondering what could have come over him all of a sudden.

'You see, Mabel, I've been thinking....'

'Yes, dear.'

'I've been thinking that up until last night I've never even raised a finger to help you with this baby.'

'That isn't true.'

'Oh yes it is. So I've decided that from now on I'm going to do *my* share of the work. I'm going to be the feed-mixer and the bottle-sterilizer. Right?'

'It's very sweet of you, dear, but I really don't think it's necessary....'

'Come on!' he cried. 'Don't change the luck! I done it the last three times and just *look* what happened! When's the next one? Two o'clock, isn't it?'

'Yes.'

'It's all mixed,' he said. 'Everything's all mixed and ready and all you've got to do when the time comes is to go out there to the larder and take it off the shelf and warm it up. That's *some* help, isn't it?'

The woman got up off her knees and went over to him and kissed him on the cheek. 'You're such a nice man,' she said. 'I love you more and more every day I know you.'

Later, in the middle of the afternoon, when Albert was outside in the sunshine working among the hives, he heard her calling to him from the house.

'Albert!' she shouted. 'Albert, come here!' She was running through the buttercups towards him.

He started forward to meet her, wondering what was wrong.

'Oh, Albert! Guess what!'

'What?'

'I've just finished giving her the two-o'clock feed and she's taken the whole lot!'

'No!'

'Every drop of it! Oh, Albert, I'm so happy! She's going to be all right! She's turned the corner just like you said!' She came up to him and threw her arms around his neck and hugged him, and he clapped her on the back and laughed and said what a marvellous little mother she was.

'Will you come in and watch the next one and see if she does it again, Albert?'

He told her he wouldn't miss it for anything, and she hugged him again, then turned and ran back to the house, skipping over the grass and singing all the way.

Naturally, there was a certain amount of suspense in the air as the time approached for the six-o'clock feed. By five thirty both parents were already seated in the living-room waiting for the moment to arrive. The bottle with the milk formula in it was standing in a saucepan of warm water on the mantelpiece. The baby was asleep in its carry-cot on the sofa.

At twenty minutes to six it woke up and started screaming its head off.

'There you are!' Mrs Taylor cried. 'She's asking for the bottle. Pick her up quick, Albert, and hand her to me here. Give me the bottle first.'

He gave her the bottle, then placed the baby on the woman's lap. Cautiously, she touched the baby's lips with the end of the nipple. The baby seized the nipple between its gums and began to suck ravenously with a rapid powerful action.

'Oh, Albert, isn't it wonderful?' she said, laughing.

'It's terrific, Mabel.'

In seven or eight minutes, the entire contents of the bottle had disappeared down the baby's throat.

'You clever girl,' Mrs Taylor said. 'Four ounces again.'

Albert Taylor was leaning forward in his chair, peering intently into the baby's face. 'You know what?' he said. 'She even seems as though she's put on a touch of weight already. What do you think?'

The mother looked down at the child.

'Don't she seem bigger and fatter to you, Mabel, than she was yesterday?'

'Maybe she does, Albert. I'm not sure. Although actually there couldn't be any *real* gain in such a short time as this. The important thing is that she's eating normally.'

'She's turned the corner,' Albert said. 'I don't think you need worry about her any more.'

'I certainly won't.'

'You want me to go up and fetch the cradle back into our own bedroom, Mabel?'

'Yes, please,' she said.

Albert went upstairs and moved the cradle. The woman followed with the baby, and after changing its nappy, she laid it gently down on its bed. Then she covered it with sheet and blanket.

'Doesn't she look lovely, Albert?' she whispered. 'Isn't that the most beautiful baby you've ever seen in your *entire* life?'

'Leave her be now, Mabel,' he said. 'Come on downstairs and cook us a bit of supper. We both deserve it.'

After they had finished eating, the parents settled themselves in armchairs in the living-room, Albert with his magazine and his pipe, Mrs Taylor with her knitting. But this was a very different scene from the one of the night before. Suddenly, all tensions had vanished. Mrs Taylor's handsome oval face was glowing with pleasure, her cheeks were pink, her eyes were sparkling bright, and her mouth was fixed in a little dreamy smile of pure content. Every now and again she would glance up from her knitting and gaze affectionately at her husband. Occasionally, she would stop the clicking of her needles altogether for a few seconds and sit quite still, looking at the ceiling, listening for a cry or a whimper from upstairs. But all was quiet.

'Albert,' she said after a while.

'Yes, dear?'

'What was it you were going to tell me last night when you came rushing up to the bedroom? You said you had an idea for the baby.'

Albert Taylor lowered the magazine on to his lap and gave her a long sly look.

'Did I?' he said.

'Yes.' She waited for him to go on, but he didn't.

'What's the big joke?' she asked. 'Why are you grinning like that?'

'It's a joke all right,' he said.

'Tell it to me, dear.'

'I'm not sure I ought to,' he said. 'You might call me a liar.'

She had seldom seen him looking so pleased with himself as he was now, and she smiled back at him, egging him on.

'I'd just like to see your face when you hear it, Mabel, that's all.'

'Albert, what *is* all this?'

He paused, refusing to be hurried.

'You do think the baby's better, don't you?' he asked.

'Of course I do.'

'You agree with me that all of a sudden she's feeding marvellously and looking one-hundred-per-cent different?'

'I do, Albert, yes.'

'That's good,' he said, the grin widening. 'You see, it's me that did it.'

'Did what?'

'I cured the baby.'

'Yes, dear, I'm sure you did.' Mrs Taylor went right on with her knitting.

'You don't believe me, do you?'

'Of course I believe you, Albert. I give you all the credit, every bit of it.'

'Then how did I do it?'

'Well,' she said, pausing a moment to think. 'I suppose it's simply that you're a brilliant feed-mixer. Ever since you started mixing the feeds she's got better and better.'

'You mean there's some sort of an art in mixing the feeds?'

'Apparently there is.' She was knitting away and smiling quietly to herself, thinking how funny men were.

'I'll tell you a secret,' he said. 'You're absolutely right. Although, mind you, it isn't so much *how* you mix it that counts. It's what you put in. You realize that, don't you, Mabel?'

Mrs Taylor stopped knitting and looked up sharply at her husband. 'Albert,' she said, 'don't tell me you've been putting things into that child's milk?'

He sat there grinning.

'Well, have you or haven't you?'

'It's possible,' he said.

'I don't believe it.'

He had a strange fierce way of grinning that showed his teeth.

'Albert,' she said. 'Stop playing with me like this.'

'Yes, dear, all right.'

'You haven't *really* put anything into her milk, have you? Answer me properly, Albert. This could be serious with such a tiny baby.'

'The answer is yes, Mabel.'

'*Albert Taylor!* How could you?'

'Now don't get excited,' he said. 'I'll tell you all about it if you really want me to, but for heaven's sake keep your hair on.'

'It was beer!' she cried. 'I just know it was beer!'

'Don't be so daft, Mabel, please.'

'Then what was it?'

Albert laid his pipe down carefully on the table beside him and leaned back in his chair. 'Tell me,' he said, 'did you ever by any chance happen to hear me mentioning something called royal jelly?'

'I did not.'

'It's magic,' he said. 'Pure magic. And last night I suddenly got the idea that if I was to put some of this into the baby's milk....'

'How *dare* you!'

'Now, Mabel, you don't even know what it is yet.'

'I don't care what it is,' she said. 'You can't go putting foreign bodies like that into a tiny baby's milk. You must be mad.'

'It's perfectly harmless, Mabel, otherwise I wouldn't have done it. It comes from bees.'

'I might have guessed that.'

'And it's so precious that practically no one can afford to take it. When they do, it's only one little drop at a time.'

'And how much did you give to our baby, might I ask?'

'Ah,' he said, 'That's the whole point. That's where the difference lies. I reckon that our baby, just in the last four feeds, has already swallowed about fifty times as much royal jelly as anyone else in the world has ever swallowed before. How about that?'

'Albert, stop pulling my leg.'

'I swear it,' he said proudly.

She sat there staring at him, her brow wrinkled, her mouth slightly open.

'You know what this stuff actually costs, Mabel, if you want to buy it? There's a place in America advertising it for sale at this very moment for something like five hundred dollars a pound jar! *Five hundred dollars!* That's more than gold, you know!'

She hadn't the faintest idea what he was talking about.

'I'll prove it,' he said, and he jumped up and went across to the large bookcase where he kept all his literature about bees. On the top shelf, the back numbers of the *American Bee Journal* were neatly stacked alongside those of the *British Bee Journal, Beecraft*, and other magazines. He took down the last issue of the *American Bee Journal* and turned to a page of small classified advertisements at the back.

'Here you are,' he said. 'Exactly as I told you. "We sell

royal jelly – $480 per lb. jar wholesale." '

He handed her the magazine so she could read it herself.

'Now do you believe me? This is an actual shop in New York, Mabel. It says so.'

'It doesn't say you can go stirring it into the milk of a practically new-born baby,' she said. 'I don't know what's come over you, Albert, I really don't.'

'It's curing her, isn't it?'

'I'm not so sure about that, now.'

'Don't be so damn silly, Mabel. You know it is.'

'Then why haven't other people done it with *their* babies?'

'I keep telling you,' he said. 'It's too expensive. Practically nobody in the world can afford to buy royal jelly just for *eating* except maybe one or two multimillionaires. The people who buy it are the big companies that make women's face creams and things like that. They're using it as a stunt. They mix a tiny pinch of it into a big jar of face cream and it's selling like hot cakes for absolutely enormous prices. They claim it takes out the wrinkles.'

'And does it?'

'Now how on earth would I know that, Mabel? Anyway,' he said, returning to his chair, 'that's not the point. The point is this. It's done so much good to our little baby just in the last few hours that I think we ought to go right on giving it to her. Now don't interrupt, Mabel. Let me finish. I've got two hundred and forty hives out there and if I turn over maybe a hundred of them to making royal jelly, we ought to be able to supply her with all she wants.'

'Albert Taylor,' the woman said, stretching her eyes wide and staring at him. 'Have you gone out of your mind?'

'Just hear me through, will you please?'

'I forbid it,' she said, 'absolutely. You're not to give my baby another drop of that horrid jelly, you understand?'

'Now, Mabel ....'

'And quite apart from that, we had a shocking honey crop last year, and if you go fooling around with those hives now, there's no telling what might not happen.'

'There's nothing wrong with my hives, Mabel.'

'You know very well we had only half the normal crop last year.'

'Do me a favour, will you?' he said. 'Let me explain some of the marvellous things this stuff does.'

'You haven't even told me what it is yet.'

'All right, Mabel. I'll do that too. Will you listen? Will you give me a chance to explain it?'

She sighed and picked up her knitting once more. 'I suppose you might as well get it off your chest, Albert. Go on and tell me.'

He paused, a bit uncertain now how to begin. It wasn't going to be easy to explain something like this to a person with no detailed knowledge of apiculture at all.

'You know, don't you,' he said, 'that each colony has only one queen?'

'Yes.'

'And that this queen lays all the eggs?'

'Yes, dear. That much I know.'

'All right. Now the queen can actually lay two different kinds of eggs. You didn't know that, but she can. It's what we call one of the miracles of the hive. She can lay eggs that produce drones, and she can lay eggs that produce workers. Now if that isn't a miracle, Mabel, I don't know what is.'

'Yes, Albert, all right.'

'The drones are the males. We don't have to worry about them. The workers are all females. So is the queen, of course. But the workers are unsexed females, if you see what I mean. Their organs are completely undeveloped, whereas the queen is tremendously sexy. She can actually lay her own weight in eggs in a single day.'

He hesitated, marshalling his thoughts.

'Now what happens is this. The queen crawls around on the comb and lays her eggs in what we call cells. You know all those hundreds of little holes you see in a honeycomb? Well, a brood comb is just about the same except the cells don't have honey in them, they have eggs. She lays one egg to each cell, and in three days each of these eggs hatches out into a tiny grub. We call it a larva.

'Now, as soon as this larva appears, the nurse bees – they're young workers – all crowd round and start feeding it like mad. And you know what they feed it on?'

'Royal jelly,' Mabel answered patiently.

'Right!' he cried. 'That's exactly what they do feed it on. They get this stuff out of a gland in their heads and they start pumping it into the cell to feed the larva. And what happens then?'

He paused dramatically, blinking at her with his small watery-grey eyes. Then he turned slowly in his chair and reached for the magazine that he had been reading the night before.

'You want to know what happens then?' he asked, wetting his lips.

'I can hardly wait.'

' "Royal jelly," ' he read aloud, ' "must be a substance of tremendous nourishing power, for on this diet alone, the honey-bee larva increases in weight *fifteen hundred times* in five days!" '

'How much?'

'*Fifteen hundred times*, Mabel. And you know what that means if you put it in terms of a human being? It means,' he said, lowering his voice, leaning forward, fixing her with those small pale eyes, 'it means that in five days a baby weighing seven and a half pounds to start off with would increase in weight to *five tons*!'

For the second time, Mrs Taylor stopped knitting.

'Now you mustn't take that too literally, Mabel.'

'Who says I mustn't?'

'It's just a scientific way of putting it, that's all.'

'Very well, Albert. Go on.'

'But that's only half the story,' he said. 'There's more to come. The really amazing thing about royal jelly, I haven't told you yet. I'm going to show you now how it can transform a plain dull-looking little worker bee with practically no sex organs at all into a great big beautiful fertile queen.'

'Are you saying our baby is dull-looking and plain?' she asked sharply.

'Now don't go putting words into my mouth, Mabel, please. Just listen to this. Did you know that the queen bee and the worker bee, although they are completely different when they grow up, are both hatched out of exactly the same kind of egg?'

'I don't believe that,' she said.

'It's true as I'm sitting here, Mabel, honest it is. Any time the bees want a queen to hatch out of the egg instead of a worker, they can do it.'

'How?'

'Ah,' he said, shaking a thick forefinger in her direction. 'That's just what I'm coming to. That's the secret of the whole thing. Now – what do *you* think it is, Mabel, that makes this miracle happen?'

'Royal jelly,' she answered. 'You already told me.'

'Royal jelly it is!' he cried, clapping his hands and bouncing up on his seat. His big round face was glowing with excitement now, and two vivid patches of scarlet had appeared high up on each cheek.

'Here's how it works. I'll put it very simply for you. The bees want a new queen. So they build an extra-large cell, a queen cell we call it, and they get the old queen to lay one of her eggs in there. The other one thousand nine hundred and ninety-nine eggs she lays in ordinary worker cells. Now. As soon as these eggs hatch into larvae, the nurse bees rally round and start pumping in the royal jelly. All of them get it, workers as well as queen. But here's the vital thing, Mabel, so listen carefully. Here's where the difference comes. The worker larvae only receive this special marvellous food for the *first three days* of their larval life. After that they have a complete change of diet. What really happens is they get weaned, except that it's not like an ordinary weaning because it's so sudden. After the third day they're put straight away on to more or less routine bees' food – a mixture of honey and pollen – and then about two weeks later they emerge from the cells as workers.

'But not so the larva in the queen cell! This one gets royal jelly *all the way through its larval life*. The nurse bees simply pour it into the cell, so much so in fact that the little larva is literally floating in it. And that's what makes it into a queen!'

'You can't prove it,' she said.

'Don't talk so damn silly, Mabel, please. Thousands of people have proved it time and time again, famous scientists in every country in the world. All you have to do is take a larva out of a worker cell and put it in a queen cell – that's what we call grafting – and just so long as the nurse bees keep it well supplied with royal jelly, then presto! – it'll grow up into a queen! And what makes it more marvellous still is the absolutely enormous difference between a queen and a worker when they grow up. The abdomen is a different shape. The sting is different. The legs are different. The ....'

'In what way are the legs different?' she asked, testing him.

'The legs? Well, the workers have little pollen baskets on their legs for carrying the pollen. The queen has none. Now here's another thing. The queen has fully developed sex organs. The workers don't. And most amazing of all, Mabel, the queen lives for an average of four to six years. The worker hardly lives that many months. And all this difference simply because one of them got royal jelly and the other didn't!'

'It's pretty hard to believe,' she said, 'that a food can do all that.'

'Of course it's hard to believe. It's another of the miracles of the hive. In fact it's the biggest ruddy miracle of them all. It's such a hell of a big miracle that it's baffled the greatest men of science for hundreds of years. Wait a moment. Stay there. Don't move.'

Again he jumped up and went over to the bookcase and started rummaging among the books and magazines.

'I'm going to find you a few of the reports. Here we are.

125

Here's one of them. Listen to this.' He started reading aloud from a copy of the *American Bee Journal*:

' "Living in Toronto at the head of a fine research laboratory given to him by the people of Canada in recognition of his truly great contribution to humanity in the discovery of insulin, Dr Frederick A. Banting became curious about royal jelly. He requested his staff to do a basic fractional analysis...." '

He paused.

'Well, there's no need to read it all, but here's what happened. Dr Banting and his people took some royal jelly from queen cells that contained two-day-old larvae, and then they started analysing it. And what d'you think they found?'

'They found,' he said, 'that royal jelly contained phenols, sterols, glycerils, dextrose, *and* − now here it comes − and eighty to eighty-five per cent *unidentified* acids!'

He stood beside the bookcase with the magazine in his hand, smiling a funny little furtive smile of triumph, and his wife watched him, bewildered.

He was not a tall man; he had a thick plump pulpy-looking body that was built close to the ground on abbreviated legs. The legs were slightly bowed. The head was huge and round, covered with bristly short-cut hair, and the greater part of the face − now that he had given up shaving altogether − was hidden by a brownish yellow fuzz about an inch long. In one way and another, he was rather grotesque to look at, there was no denying that.

'Eighty to eighty-five per cent,' he said, 'unidentified acids. Isn't that fantastic?' He turned back to the bookshelf and began hunting through the other magazines.

'What does it mean, unidentified acids?'

'That's the whole point! No one knows! Not even Banting could find out. You've heard of Banting?'

'No.'

'He just happens to be about the most famous living doctor in the world today, that's all.'

Looking at him now as he buzzed around in front of the

bookcase with his bristly head and his hairy face and his plump pulpy body, she couldn't help thinking that somehow, in some curious way, there was a touch of the bee about this man. She had often seen women grow to look like the horses that they rode, and she had noticed that people who bred birds or bull terriers or pomeranians frequently resembled in some small but startling manner the creature of their choice. But up until now it had never occurred to her that her husband might look like a bee. It shocked her a bit.

'And did Banting ever try to eat it,' she asked, 'this royal jelly?'

'Of course he didn't eat it, Mabel. He didn't have enough for that. It's too precious.'

'You know something?' she said, staring at him but smiling a little all the same. 'You're getting to look just a teeny bit like a bee yourself, did you know that?'

He turned and looked at her.

'I suppose it's the beard mostly,' she said. 'I do wish you'd stop wearing it. Even the colour is sort of bee-ish, don't you think?'

'What the hell are you talking about, Mabel?'

'Albert,' she said. 'Your language.'

'Do you want to hear any more of this or don't you?'

'Yes, dear, I'm sorry. I was only joking. Do go on.'

He turned away again and pulled another magazine out of the bookcase and began leafing through the pages. 'Now just listen to this, Mabel. "In 1939, Heyl experimented with twenty-one-day-old rats, injecting them with royal jelly in varying amounts. As a result, he found a precocious follicular development of the ovaries directly in proportion to the quantity of royal jelly injected." '

'There!' she cried. 'I knew it!'

'Knew what?'

'I knew something terrible would happen.'

'Nonsense. There's nothing wrong with that. Now here's another, Mabel. "Still and Burdett found that a male rat which hitherto had been unable to breed, upon receiving a minute daily dose of royal jelly, became a father many times over." '

'Albert,' she cried, 'this stuff is *much* too strong to give to a baby! I don't like it at all.'

'Nonsense, Mabel.'

'Then why do they only try it out on rats, tell me that? Why don't some of these famous scientists take it themselves? They're too clever, that's why. Do you think Dr Banting is going to risk finishing up with precious ovaries? Not him.'

'But they *have* given it to people, Mabel. Here's a whole article about it. Listen.' He turned the page and again began reading from the magazine. ' "In Mexico, in 1953, a group of enlightened physicians began prescribing minute doses of royal jelly for such things as cerebral neuritis, arthritis, diabetes, autointoxication from tobacco, impotence in men, asthma, croup, and gout.... There are stacks of signed testimonials.... A celebrated stockbroker in Mexico City contracted a particularly stubborn case of psoriasis. He became physically unattractive. His clients began to forsake him. His business began to suffer. In desperation he turned to royal jelly – one drop with every meal – and presto! – he was cured in a fortnight. A waiter in the Café Jena, also in Mexico City, reported that his father, after taking minute doses of this wonder substance in capsule form, sired a healthy boy child at the age of ninety. A bullfight promoter in Acapulco, finding himself landed with a rather lethargic-looking bull, injected it with one gramme of royal jelly (an excessive dose) just before it entered the arena. Thereupon, the beast became so swift and savage that it promptly dispatched two picadors, three horses, and a matador, and finally...." '

'Listen!' Mrs Taylor said, interrupting him. 'I think the baby's crying.'

Albert glanced up from his reading. Sure enough, a lusty yelling noise was coming from the bedroom above.

'She must be hungry,' he said.

His wife looked at the clock. 'Good gracious me!' she cried, jumping up. 'It's past her time again already! You mix the feed, Albert, quickly, while I bring her down! But hurry! I don't want to keep her waiting.'

In half a minute, Mrs Taylor was back, carrying the screaming infant in her arms. She was flustered now, still quite unaccustomed to the ghastly nonstop racket that a healthy baby makes when it wants its food. 'Do be quick, Albert!' she called, settling herself in the armchair and arranging the child on her lap. 'Please hurry!'

Albert entered from the kitchen and handed her the bottle of warm milk. 'It's just right,' he said. 'You don't have to test it.'

She hitched the baby's head a little higher in the crook of her arm, then pushed the rubber teat straight into the wide-open yelling mouth. The baby grabbed the teat and began to suck. The yelling stopped. Mrs Taylor relaxed.

'Oh, Albert, isn't she lovely?'

'She's terrific, Mabel — thanks to royal jelly.'

'Now, dear, I don't want to hear another word about that nasty stuff. It frightens me to death.'

'You're making a big mistake,' he said.

'We'll see about that.'

The baby went on sucking the bottle.

'I do believe she's going to finish the whole lot again, Albert.'

'I'm sure she is,' he said.

And a few minutes later, the milk was all gone.

'Oh, what a good girl you are!' Mrs Taylor cried, as very gently she started to withdraw the nipple. The baby sensed what she was doing and sucked harder, trying to hold on. The woman gave a quick little tug, and *plop*, out it came.

'Waa! Waa! Waa! Waa! Waa!' the baby yelled.

'Nasty old wind,' Mrs Taylor said, hoisting the child on to her shoulder and patting its back.

It belched twice in quick succession.

'There you are, my darling, you'll be all right now.'

For a few seconds, the yelling stopped. Then it started again.

'Keep belching her,' Albert said. 'She's drunk it too quick.'

His wife lifted the baby back on to her shoulder. She rubbed its spine. She changed it from one shoulder to the other. She lay it on its stomach on her lap. She sat it up on her knee. But it didn't belch again, and the yelling became louder and more insistent every minute.

'Good for the lungs,' Albert Taylor said, grinning. 'That's the way they exercise their lungs, Mabel, did you know that?'

'There, there, there,' the wife said, kissing it all over the face. 'There, there, there.'

They waited another five minutes, but not for one moment did the screaming stop.

'Change the nappy,' Albert said. 'It's got a wet nappy, that's all it is.' He fetched a clean one from the kitchen, and Mrs Taylor took the old one off and put the new one on.

This made no difference at all.

'Waa! Waa! Waa! Waa! Waa!' the baby yelled.

'You didn't stick the safety pin through the skin, did you, Mabel?'

'Of course I didn't,' she said, feeling under the nappy with her fingers to make sure.

The parents sat opposite one another in their armchairs, smiling nervously, watching the baby on the mother's lap, waiting for it to tire and stop screaming.

'You know what?' Albert Taylor said at last.

'What?'

'I'll bet she's still hungry. I'll bet all she wants is another swig at that bottle. How about me fetching her an extra lot?'

'I don't think we ought to do that, Albert.'

'It'll do her good,' he said, getting up from his chair. 'I'm going to warm her up a second helping.'

He went into the kitchen, and was away several minutes. When he returned he was holding a bottle brimful of milk.

'I made her a double,' he announced. 'Eight ounces. Just in case.'

'Albert! Are you mad? Don't you know it's just as bad to overfeed as it is to underfeed?'

'You don't have to give her the lot, Mabel. You can stop any time you like. Go on,' he said, standing over her. 'Give her a drink.'

Mrs Taylor began to tease the baby's upper lip with the end of the nipple. The tiny mouth closed like a trap over the rubber teat and suddenly there was silence in the room. The baby's whole body relaxed and a look of absolute bliss came over its face as it started to drink.

'There you are, Mabel! What did I tell you?'

The woman didn't answer.

'She's ravenous, that's what she is. Just look at her suck.'

Mrs Taylor was watching the level of the milk in the bottle. It was dropping fast, and before long three or four ounces out of the eight had disappeared.

'There,' she said. 'That'll do.'

'You can't pull it away now, Mabel.'

'Yes, dear. I must.'

'Go on, woman. Give her the rest and stop fussing.'

'But *Albert* ...'

'She's famished, can't you see that? Go on, my beauty,' he said. 'You finish that bottle.'

'I don't like it, Albert,' the wife said, but she didn't pull the bottle away.

'She's making up for lost time, Mabel, that's all she's doing.'

Five minutes later the bottle was empty. Slowly, Mrs Taylor withdrew the nipple, and this time there was no protest from the baby, no sound at all. It lay peacefully on the mother's lap, the eyes glazed with contentment, the mouth half-open, the lips smeared with milk.

'Twelve whole ounces, Mabel!' Albert Taylor said. 'Three times the normal amount! Isn't that amazing!'

The woman was staring down at the baby. And now the old anxious tight-lipped look of the frightened mother was slowly returning to her face.

'What's the matter with *you*?' Albert asked. 'You're not worried by that, are you? You can't expect her to get back to normal on a lousy four ounces, don't be ridiculous.'

'Come here, Albert,' she said.

'What?'

'I said come here.'

He went over and stood beside her.

'Take a good look and tell me if you see anything different.'

He peered closely at the baby. 'She seems bigger, Mabel, if that's what you mean. Bigger and fatter.'

'Hold her,' she ordered. 'Go on, pick her up.'

He reached out and lifted the baby up off the mother's lap. 'Good God!' he cried. 'She weighs a ton!'

'Exactly.'

'Now isn't that marvellous!' he cried, beaming. 'I'll bet she must be back to normal already!'

'It frightens me, Albert. It's too quick.'

'Nonsense, woman.'

'It's that disgusting jelly that's done it,' she said. 'I hate the stuff.'

'There's nothing disgusting about royal jelly,' he answered, indignant.

'Don't be a fool, Albert! You think it's *normal* for a child to start putting on weight at this speed?'

'You're never satisfied!' he cried. 'You're scared stiff when she's losing and now you're absolutely terrified because she's gaining! What's the matter with you, Mabel?'

The woman got up from her chair with the baby in her arms and started towards the door. 'All I can say is,' she said, 'it's lucky I'm here to see you don't give her any more of it, that's all I can say.' She went out, and Albert watched her through the open door as she crossed the hall to the foot of the stairs and started to ascend, and when she reached the third or fourth step she suddenly stopped and stood quite still for several seconds as though remembering something. Then she turned and came down again rather quickly and re-entered the room.

'Albert,' she said.

'Yes?'

'I assume there wasn't any royal jelly in this last feed we've just given her?'

'I don't see why you should assume that, Mabel.'

'Albert!'

'What's wrong?' he asked, soft and innocent.

'How *dare* you!' she cried.

Albert Taylor's great bearded face took on a pained and puzzled look. 'I think you ought to be very glad she's got another big dose of it inside her,' he said. 'Honest I do. And this *is* a big dose, Mabel, believe you me.'

The woman was standing just inside the doorway clasping the sleeping baby in her arms and staring at her husband with huge eyes. She stood very erect, her body absolutely stiff with fury, her face paler, more tight-lipped than ever.

'You mark my words,' Albert was saying, 'you're going to have a nipper there soon that'll win first prize in any baby show in the *entire* country. Hey, why don't you weigh her now and see what she is? You want me to get the scales, Mabel, so you can weigh her?'

The woman walked straight over to the large table in the centre of the room and laid the baby down and quickly started taking off its clothes. 'Yes!' she snapped. 'Get the scales!' Off came the little nightgown, then the undervest.

Then she unpinned the nappy and she drew it away and the baby lay naked on the table.

'But Mabel!' Albert cried. 'It's a miracle! She's fat as a puppy!'

Indeed, the amount of flesh the child had put on since the day before was astounding. The small sunken chest with the rib bones showing all over it was now plump and round as a barrel, and the belly was bulging high in the air. Curiously, though, the arms and legs did not seem to have grown in proportion. Still short and skinny, they looked like little sticks protruding from a ball of fat.

'Look!' Albert said. 'She's even beginning to get a bit of fuzz on her tummy to keep her warm!' He put out a hand and was about to run the tips of his fingers over the powdering of silky yellowy-brown hairs that had suddenly appeared on the baby's stomach.

'*Don't you touch her!*' the woman cried. She turned and faced him, her eyes blazing, and she looked suddenly like some kind of little fighting bird with her neck arched over towards him as though she were about to fly at his face and peck his eyes out.

'Now wait a minute,' he said, retreating.

'You must be mad!' she cried.

'Now wait just one minute, Mabel, will you please, because if you're still thinking this stuff is dangerous ... That *is* what you're thinking, isn't it? All right, then. Listen carefully. I shall now proceed to *prove* to you once and for all, Mabel, that royal jelly is absolutely harmless to human beings, even in enormous doses. For example – why do you think we had only half the usual honey crop last summer? Tell me that.'

His retreat, walking backwards, had taken him three or four yards away from her, where he seemed to feel more comfortable.

'The reason we had only half the usual crop last summer,' he said slowly, lowering his voice, 'was because I turned one hundred of my hives over to the production of royal jelly.'

'You *what?*'

'Ah,' he whispered. 'I thought that might surprise you a bit. And I've been making it ever since right under your very nose.' His small eyes were glinting at her, and a slow sly smile was creeping around the corners of his mouth.

'You'll never guess the reason, either,' he said. 'I've been afraid to mention it up to now because I thought it might ... well ... sort of embarrass you.'

There was a slight pause. He had his hands clasped high in front of him, level with his chest, and he was rubbing one palm against the other, making a soft scraping noise.

'You remember that bit I read you out of the magazine? That bit about the rat? Let me see now, how does it go? "Still and Burdett found that a male rat which hitherto had been unable to breed ..." ' He hesitated, the grin widening, showing his teeth.

'You get the message, Mabel?'

She stood quite still, facing him.

'The very first time I ever read that sentence, Mabel, I jumped straight out of my chair and I said to myself if it'll work with a lousy rat, I said, there's no reason on earth why it shouldn't work with Albert Taylor.'

He paused again, craning his head forward and turning one ear slightly in his wife's direction, waiting for her to say something. But she didn't.

'And here's another thing,' he went on. 'It made me feel so absolutely marvellous, Mabel, and so sort of completely different to what I was before that I went right on taking it even after you'd announced the joyful tidings. *Buckets* of it I must have swallowed during the last twelve months.'

The big heavy haunted-looking eyes of the woman were moving intently over the man's face and neck. There was no skin showing at all on the neck, not even at the sides below the ears. The whole of it, to a point where it disappeared into the collar of the shirt, was covered all the way around with those shortish silky hairs, yellowy black.

'Mind you,' he said, turning away from her, gazing lovingly now at the baby, 'it's going to work far better on a tiny infant than on a fully developed man like me. You've only got to look at her to see that, don't you agree?'

The woman's eyes travelled slowly downward and settled on the baby. The baby was lying naked on the table, fat and white and comatose, like some gigantic grub that was approaching the end of its larval life and would soon emerge into the world complete with mandibles and wings.

'Why don't you cover her up, Mabel?' he said. 'We don't want our little queen to catch a cold.'

Titles in the WLE Short Stories series